ALLIGATOR, ROOM 8

GATOR-MAN #2

Other Books by David R. Michael

Gator-Man
Alligator Bait

Novels
Closing Crew
Gunwitch: A Tale of the King's Coven
Gunwitch: The Witch Hunts
Now Serving Dragon
The Door to the Sky
The Summoning Fire

Collections
Brain Freeze & Other Stories
Demon Candy
Dragons of the Stars
The World Wears Thin

ALLIGATOR, ROOM 8
GATOR-MAN #2

DAVID R. MICHAEL

Published By
Four Crows Landing

For Bloody Barnabas

1

ASH TURNER WANTED nothing more than to leave New Orleans—

No, that wasn't true. There was something—someone—he wanted more, but he didn't want to—he didn't dare to—think about—

Jamie.

He gritted his teeth and didn't think about her.

What he did instead, mustering his available willpower and fortifying it with the accumulated prelunch boredom of nearly a week spent stuck in a cheap motel room, was run his first bath of the day.

Hot water—or as hot as the Tony & Cleo Motel's chugging, rattling fixtures could provide—came up to his ankles when he stepped into the too-short tub, and covered his legs when he sat down and leaned back. The broken tiles of the wall were cold against his bare skin and more than a few shifted within the crumbling constraints of their grout, but for the moment he had his own private pool.

He could have filled the tub so the water reached his lower chest when he sat in it—the tub wasn't short that

1

way—but if he filled the tub, the average temperature of the water would be merely tepid, having drained or simply overtaxed the motel's water heater.

He closed his eyes and used cupped hands to splash warm water on his chest and stomach, then on his face and shoulders. The chlorine in the water stung his nose but also obscured the warm, musty smell stirred up and pushed around by the room's ancient window-mounted heater.

He tried not to think about his room, either.

Room 8 of the Tony & Cleo Motel of New Orleans was a small, roach-infested shithole in a slightly-less-small, totally roach-infested shithole of a motel. The smooth fiberglass of the tub he sat in and the cracked tiles of the bathroom wall he leaned against were probably the cleanest, most sanitary parts of the entire establishment.

On the first day of his stay, within minutes of being shown to his room by Detective Marand and "Tony," the motel manager, Ash had walked to the nearest RiteAid and purchased more cleaning supplies than the young woman from Room 6—the so-called maid—brought with her on her so-called daily rounds. Because though a growing part of Ash would find contentment laying in muddy bayou water under the late winter sun, even that part had refused to step a naked foot into the bathtub before he cleaned it. That had been five gray, rainy, February days ago.

Ash sighed. If he got any more bored, he might take the maid up on her at least half-joking offer of sex for his "secret" of getting the tub and tiles so clean. She had stolen his spray bottle of hydrogen peroxide cleaner the day before—along with the coins he had been dumping on the nightstand by his room's single bed. So maybe she was taking her education in the cleaning arts into her own hands. Which was just as well. There was only one woman—

Ash let his head fall back and hit the tiles, threatening the integrity of the bathroom wall in order to achieve a solid thump of scalp and skull against ceramic, to derail that thought.

It was taking more effort with each passing day to keep his mind off his... obsession? His compulsion? His god-given purpose—curse—? His Jamie—

He lifted his head and smashed it back hard enough to hurt this time, and loud enough to elicit a thumping response from the motel occupant in Room 18 on the other side of the wall.

Jamie Derouen wasn't his anymore. She had never been his, no matter what either of them might have thought at the time. She had belonged to someone—*something*—else, all along.

Ash grimaced, more from the effort of will to stop thinking about her than from the pain in the back of his head. It was hard to keep his mind clear, to *not* think, during the long days of what he had taken to calling his "motel arrest."

The baths helped, as did the walks to the tiny, hole-in-the-wall sandwich shop for his lunch and dinner. That is, so long as it wasn't raining. When he walked in the rain, he could feel the eyes of the bayou watching him in spite of the black umbrella he hid beneath.

But there were only so many hot baths he could take in a day—the Tony & Cleo Motel's water heater was pushed to its meager limits to give him three—and the walk to the sandwich shop was as short as its menu, even in the rain. The rest of his day he had to fill by watching local TV stations or laying on the sagging bed of his motel room staring at the ceiling and ignoring the overheard conversations and activities of the other occupants.

Detective Marand had put Ash in Room 8 of the Tony & Cleo Motel because Ash had had nowhere to stay in town, and because the detective didn't want him to leave New Orleans. At the moment, Ash's room and board were a minor expense in the ongoing investigation of the disappearance—and possible murder—of local pillar of the community—and suspected crime boss—James Rémy Derouen.

Ash didn't know what else he could tell the detective—or anyone else in the NOPD—about the "disappearance" of James Rémy Derouen. How many different ways could Ash describe a giant alligator—walking upright—smashing into the house where Ash had been taken and held captive. Then picking up James Rémy Derouen in its claws, eating the man in two bites with a mouth the size of a small car whose make and model Ash could no longer recall, before disappearing into the swamp again?

Ash stopped splashing the warm water on his face and body. The drops suddenly reminded him of the warm blood that had rained down in the aftermath of James Derouen's messy end. He flexed his arms as if to prove they weren't strapped down, as they had been that night. He had been a captive audience, first for James Derouen's rantings, then for the man's...

Ash gave his cheeks a light slap. To distract himself again.

He tried not to think of James Derouen, because thinking of the man inevitably led to thinking about the man's daughter.

Ash had never once used the word "god" to describe the giant alligator in any of the statements he had given. If he had, he suspected where he would be staying wouldn't allow walks off site to buy his lunch, or so many daily baths. Though it might have fewer roaches.

But *god* was the correct word. "Giant alligator" was a merely description of that god. As was "angry." And "hungry."

And "watching."

Ash forced himself to relax. To feel the warm water embrace him. To let his legs bob in the water. To clear his mind.

He had to get out of New Orleans. Away from the city and the swamps that surrounded it. There was nothing for him here. No one who even knew his name, except Detective Marand and...

Jamie.

He took a breath, then bent his knees so his torso and head could slide beneath the water. His nostrils squeezed closed to keep the water out without any conscious suggestion from him to do so. He tried not think about that, too, as he let his arms float beside him.

It was easier to bear thoughts of Jamie when he was under water. His fingers twitched when he thought of her, as they always did, creating little disturbances that he could feel on his face and neck and chest. But submerged like this, he didn't have to clench his fists to quell the conflicting urges. He could almost see her, as if he could open his eyes and look up and she would be there. Her long black hair, her brown eyes, her smile. Visible but obscured by refraction and the movement of the water. Right there, but just out of reach.

Because she needed to stay out of his reach.

Floating like this, he could almost forget that he could never actually see her again.

He needed to get out of New Orleans. Because Jamie was in New Orleans. Because Jamie Derouen *was* New Orleans as far he was concerned. She had brought the city alive for him, or brought him back to life in the city. Before he was dragged out of the city and into the swamp by a couple of her father's goons, then shot in the back of the head.

Ash moved his right hand, placed it over his heart. So he could feel his heartbeat.

He remembered the bright, hot agony of dying.

He remembered the cold hell of being dead in the black water, of having his soul gnawed on by unseen teeth and manipulated by an unseen tongue and claws.

He remembered crawling up out of the swamp and stumbling back into New Orleans to discover a year had passed.

He remembered all of this, but could remember very little of his life *before*. Except Jamie. And he had no clear idea of why he was alive. Except—

He pressed his hand against the warm flesh of his chest. He didn't know how he could be alive. But the evidence was there. His heart beat. His blood moved in his veins. The air in his lungs exchanged oxygen for carbon dioxide.

He was alive. Even after James Derouen had tried to have him killed a second time.

He was alive. And as long as he was alive, Jamie Derouen, the woman he loved—had loved—-was in danger. His fists clenched, causing the fingernails of his right hand to gouge his chest.

Whatever she might have known about the agreement her father had made with the alligator god, she didn't know about the new Ash Turner. She didn't know she should stay away.

He was her doom. He knew that now.

The eyes of the bayou were watching him, waiting for him to fulfill his new purpose.

Ash planted his feet against the far end of the tub and pushed. His head and body came up out of the water as his legs straightened.

He had to leave New Orleans.

2

Detective Marand would be upset, to say the least. Maybe leaving town after a police detective told you not to leave was a crime. Maybe he really was under "motel arrest." Ash didn't know. In his life before his death, he hadn't been a lawyer.

The scratchy towels left by the so-called maid might have been white once, but, like the rest of the Tony & Cleo Motel of New Orleans, had picked up a layer of gray-beige dinge. Ash felt more scrubbed but less clean after using the towel to dry off. He dropped it on the floor of the bathroom when he was finished, so the roaches could take their turn at it, and so the maid would know he needed a new one.

He barely glanced at himself in the steamy mirror of the vanity. For all that his soul and his memories felt as if they had been ripped, shredded, and chewed on before being hastily stitched back together, his body—which had been shot—looked in remarkably good shape.

He was thirty-two years old, or had been thirty-two. Maybe he was thirty-three now? He couldn't remember his birthday, which made him wonder if he was going to be thirty-two for the rest of his life.

He was pale. He had always been pale—he remembered that—with whatever nonwhite ancestry he might have had—but could no longer remember—leaving only a slight trace in how he tanned. He had no tan now, though. Being dead in a swamp for a year and coming back to life under the gray skies of New Orleans in late February had left him ghost-like.

His brown hair was short but shaggy. He needed a haircut, as anyone would, he figured, in similar circumstances. He had been about to get a haircut six days ago, before James Derouen's goons, Sneer and Big Man, had grabbed him off the street for a second chance at killing him.

He picked up his clothes from the bed where he had left them, shaking them out before pulling them back on.

The first part of leaving would be easy, as he had almost nothing to pack. The clothes Ash had died in, and had been wearing while witnessing the gruesome death of James Derouen, had been cut off him and bagged for evidence, so the largesse of Detective Marand and the City of New Orleans provided the only luggage he had. Detective Marand had taken him on a brief shopping trip before installing him at the motel, so Ash had one pair of jeans, two tee-shirts emblazoned with the colorful logo of the most recent Mardi Gras season, two pairs of boxers, a half-dozen white socks, the cheapest pair of Converse knock offs Ash had ever worn, and an even cheaper collapsible black umbrella already on the verge of breaking. He still had the white shopping bags, so he shook one of those out, added the articles of clothing he wasn't wearing, and he was ready to go.

The second part would be more challenging. He hoped he would be able to buy a bus ticket back home—

Home?

The broken and scattered shards of his memories offered glimpses and thoughts, a jumble of images and impressions that might have been *home*. Disconnected bits of first-person experiences, most of them involving flat, glowing screens of varying sizes with freeze-frames of games, movies and source code on them. Faces. Was one of those faces his mother? He didn't know. One of the faces was of his wife—his *ex*-wife; he remembered that much—but with no name and a conflicting mélange of both positive and negative emotions. And he remembered a house. Where he had lived. That must have been his home? In...

Detective Marand had told him he was from Bixby, Oklahoma.

Ashley Turner of Bixby, Oklahoma. The one who came back.

Ash wasn't sure he could find Bixby, Oklahoma, on a map, but that didn't matter. The bus driver would know where to take him.

Assuming he could buy a bus ticket without his ID. His wallet and driver's license, like most of his past, had been lost in the swamp.

And assuming the sixty-ish dollars he had left from the "lunch money" Detective Marand had given him would suffice to buy a ticket.

That is, once he found—and walked to—a bus station. He couldn't afford a taxi, and there was no one he could call to ask for a ride. The motel room had a phone, but Ash knew no numbers except Detective Marand's.

He clenched his fists and refused to think about the other number he didn't know. The only number he wanted to know.

The room didn't have a local telephone directory, but Ash had seen one on the counter in the motel office.

Ash cast a last, quick glance around the motel room, a habit he vaguely remembered from what might be fragments of vacations, making sure he hadn't forgotten anything. He could feel a muscle memory, almost a pull, to get down on his hands and knees to look under the full-sized bed. But there was no way he wanted to see what was under there.

He considered leaving a note for the so-called maid, letting her know she was welcome to the rest of his cleaning supplies, but decided she would figure it out on her own.

He thought about leaving a note for the detective, but the man was a detective. He would figure out what had happened. He would probably even guess where Ash had gone.

Ash turned his back on the room. He tied the handles of his white plastic "luggage" to secure it from any would-be stowaways, then hung it from the knob of his door. He picked up the umbrella from where it lay looking like a dead spider by the door. He opened the door, stepped out, and pulled it closed behind him, the way he always did.

It wasn't raining at the moment, but he kept the umbrella. He didn't trust the clouds.

The New Orleans winter, with spring edging closer, was wet and gray. Lingering memories of winters further north made Ash hesitate to call it "cold." If he had a jacket, he would hardly notice the temperature. Dressed as he was, though, with only jeans and a tee-shirt, the walk would be chilly, and slow. He might not think of the temperature as cold, but he seemed to feel it more than he used to. He walked slower in the cold, as if it made his muscles stiff.

The Tony and Cleo Motel was a narrow wooden structure, with a cratered parking lot wrapped around three sides. Its twenty rooms were built back to back in a single line, terminated at the north end with the motel office. Rooms 1 through 10, clearly visible from the motel office, faced west. Rooms 11 through 20 could only be reached by walking around the motel. A sign hung inside the window of the motel office stated in no uncertain terms that hourly rates were *not* available. That there were thirty parking spaces marked in chipped and faded paint for the twenty rooms made a different, if not entirely contradictory, statement.

Behind the grimy window of the motel office, past the sign about hourly rates, Ash saw "Tony" look up, see him, then go back to watching the morning soap operas. Ash had no doubt Detective Marand had chosen Room 8 for him because the manager would be able to see when Ash came and went.

Ash turned to walk along the cracked sidewalk that separated the parking spaces from the rooms. With the rusted rear ends of combined heating and cooling units sticking out the windows, the sidewalk seemed even narrower.

The door of Room 6, where the so-called maid lived with the man she called "Daddy," was open. The so-called maid leaned against the doorframe, smoking. She wore tight stretch jeans that emphasized how thin her legs were, black sneaker wedges that boosted her well over average height, and an oversized hooded sweatshirt emblazoned with the letters "UNO" that hung on her bony shoulders and elbows. She had the hood pushed back so it hung behind her with her thick, curly dark hair. Her eyes were so brown they were nearly black, darker than her complexion.

The girl nodded to Ash when their eyes met and gave him a smile that was more in her eyes than the corners of her mouth. After offering to swap sex for cleaning tips and being awkwardly refused, she had had little to say to Ash, but always seemed to find something about him amusing. Then she pursed her lips around the cigarette she held in right hand and took a long drag. She turned her head so the smoke she released drifted away from the open door behind her, and away from Ash.

Ash nodded back. He guessed her age around twenty. Or he hoped she was at least twenty. After five days spent at the Tony and Cleo Motel, he knew how she paid the weekly rent for "Daddy," and how she kept the man in beer and Po Boys. Working as a maid was clearly a low-priority second job. Or a third job, since she seemed to have another obligation that occupied her mornings and afternoons, as well. She must have just returned from wherever that was, since her makeup was still fresh. The banged-up, four-door sedan "Daddy" drove wasn't parked in the space in front of the door.

Ash had learned the so-called maid's name from over-heard arguments with "Daddy." Daddy always bellowed it out: "Kayla!" Usually followed by something along the lines of: "You get your skinny ass back in here!" Or: "You get your bony ass out of that bathroom and you tell me that to my face!" But since Ash and she hadn't been properly introduced, Ash was reluctant to use her name or refer to her by it. He didn't want to embarrass her. Or himself.

"I think you all have a visitor, Room 8," the girl said, surprising him. She nodded to indicate something or someone across the street. Her voice was low and, to Ash's ear, heavily accented. Gulf Coast Southern, but with the specific sound of New Orleans. "I'm pretty sure she's not here for me."

He stopped. "A visitor?"

She nodded again, and gestured with her cigarette. "A lady this time," she said, with an odd emphasis on the word *lady*. "Pretty, and probably rich, going off her car. Not some crusty old policeman. You all are moving up in the world, Room 8."

His heart started beating faster as he followed her gaze to see a sleek, low-slung red sports car—some part of his mind insisted he knew the make, model and year, but offered no specifics, just as it had with Daddy's car—parked on the street across from the motel. The windows were tinted black and he couldn't see through to whoever might be waiting in the car.

The last time he had been surprised by a vehicle, it had been a minivan full of men in dark suits with Tasers and zip ties.

As he looked, the driver's door of the car swung open and a woman stepped out. Like the so-called maid, the woman wore stretch jeans and an oversized gray hooded sweatshirt, but of much more expensive design, and she had on gray boots that came to her knees. She wore her long hair back in a gray silk scarf, and half her face was covered by black sunglasses that matched the curve and shape of the windows in the sports car. All he could see of her face was her lips—

Recognition hit him like a combination of a punch to the mouth and being tasered in the back of the neck. His heart jolted and threatened to burst out of his ribcage. He staggered. From the blow and from the conflicting urges to run to her and from her.

"Jamie," he managed to whisper with what was left of the breath knocked out of him. He stepped toward her on shaky legs. He dropped the umbrella and his hands came up, stretching toward her. His motions were jerky, like those of a puppet controlled by a toddler.

He couldn't read the expression on Jamie's face. Her eyes were large gray mirrors of the clouds overhead and her lips were pressed together.

Ash tasted the dirty water of the bayou. He thought he heard a thunder of laughter behind the clouds overhead.

"Jamie!" he shouted. He pulled his hands to his chest. His fingers were tense, curled like claws in anticipation of being able to grab her and pull her close, where he could smell her and taste her—

He loved her. He needed her.

And if she came too close, he would kill her. He wouldn't be able to stop himself.

He would tear out her throat with his teeth and rake the flesh of her back her with his claws—

A scattering of raindrops fell around Ash, pushed by the rising wind. If any drops touched him, he didn't feel them. He focused on Jamie.

He saw her lips part as she paused in the middle of the street, just beyond the dark spots the rain had made on the asphalt. "Ash?"

Her voice was a siren's call. A lure to a death trap. Hers and his.

Ash realized he had tripped over his own feet and fallen to his knees. The rough surface of the asphalt scraped painfully against his knees, providing a distraction from the overwhelming compulsion that had erupted inside him at the sight of Jamie Derouen, the woman he loved. Had loved, before—

The woman he had to kill—

Because the alligator god insisted—

Ash pressed his clawed fingers against the sides of his head. His fingers remained stiff, curled, and he was probably drawing blood from his scalp, but ten points of additional pain granted him additional clarity.

He had to—

"Ash? What's going on?"

He had to get away—

The tone of the thunder became threatening. More rain fell and this time Ash felt the cold drops on his skin. Behind him, he heard the so-called maid step away from her open door. "Are you OK, Room 8?"

In front of him, raindrops slashing dark stripes down the front of her shirt, Jamie stepped from the street to the parking lot of the Tony & Cleo Motel. The world seemed to tilt toward Jamie. As if the world itself were trying to throw him at her.

He twisted around and scrambled uphill, away from Jamie, on his hands and knees. Room 8 was too far away, and the door was locked. The door of Room 6, however, was open in front of him.

He crawled through a shallow puddle that was quickly refilling as more rain fell. The so-called maid shouted in surprise and dropped her cigarette as she dodged out of his way before he could knock her down at the knees and crawl over her. Then he was inside Room 6 and had pushed the door closed. The automatic locked clicked into place.

He grabbed the doorknob to pull himself up, but his fingers were suddenly too long and jointed wrong. He struggled to get a grip. Finally he was able to get to his feet by pushing against the door, his rubber-soled shoes creating ripples in the old, limp carpet and nearly ripping it. His fingernails carved grooves in the paint on the metal door as he fumbled with the chain latch, but his fingers were too long and clumsy to make it work. He turned and collapsed with his back against the door, bracing with his feet on the worn carpeting.

"God damn it, Room 8!" the so-called maid shouted as she hit the door. "You are not locking me out of my own room!"

Ash jumped at the impact on the door behind him. He looked around the room, hoping for a way out that he knew wasn't there. No light was on, and the curtains were drawn, but a three-wick candle burning on the nightstand showed him the details of the room. Just like his room, Room 6 shared a back wall with the room behind it. There was only the one door and one window, both at the front.

Unlike his room, though, Room 6 had two beds. The bed nearest the door was neatly made, with its faded floral bedspread pulled tight and its pillows tucked in, ready for turndown service. The other bed was a rat's nest of discarded beer cans and rumpled clothes piled against the wall and showing the distinct impression where a large man had lain to watch TV and sleep. The rat's nest spilled over to cover most of the back half of the room, with a barely visible path to the door of the bathroom. The candle on the nightstand between the two beds created a blanket of vanilla fog that failed to completely smother the stale scents of spilled beer, leftover takeout, cigarette smoke, and sweaty man funk.

Ash coughed and blew out through his stinging, burning nose. It didn't help, so he let his nostrils squeeze closed the way they always did under water. Despite the stinging in his eyes, no tears came. He blinked. The stinging stopped, but now it was as if he were looking at the room through a window, or wore protective goggles.

The so-called maid banged on the door again. Then he heard her trying to get her key into the lock. He heard the footsteps of another woman approaching the door. He didn't have to see the woman to know it was Jamie. This close, her presence burned in his mind.

"Ash!" Jamie shouted at the same time he heard the key pushed into the lock. Then softer. "Ash?"

"No!" Ash shouted, the word torn out of his chest through his throat from the effort required not to open the door and pull her to him. "Go away! You can't—"

He brought his hands up to hide his face—

As if he had been goaded with a cattle prod directly to his brain, he jerked upright and stumbled away from the door, staring at his hands. Gray scales covered his palms and the backs of his hands, and continued up his arms. Webbing connected his fingers, which were now tipped with long, gray-black claws.

Twin images flashed in his mind and threatened to tear him apart. Jamie recoiling in horror from the sight of what he had become. Jamie's blood on his hands as he grabbed her and pulled her to him, his claws sinking into her flesh as he opened his mouth impossibly wide—

He fell to his knees, his legs again doing what they could to keep him away from Jamie even as he twisted at the waist, his clawed hands reaching out for her. Inches from the tips of his claws, the doorknob twisted.

Beyond the door, Jamie said his name again.

He choked on her name, refusing to say it.

"Go away!" he managed to say. "You have to go away!"

The door opened, a vertical line of gray light that threatened to expose him for the monster he had become.

"Go away!"

He threw himself to the floor, and crawled on his stomach under the bed nearest the door.

3

THE CLAWS ON Ash's fingers caught on the bedspread, so he dragged it with him as he crawled under the bed. He felt the bedspread pulling the sheets and the two pillows with it as he pushed forward. With the bedspread wrapping itself tight around him, the darkness under the bed was nearly complete. He couldn't even see the dusty carpet in front of his face.

The door to the room slammed open.

"What the hell are you doing?" the so-called maid shouted.

"Ash!"

He felt a hand grab his right ankle. He shook it off, losing his sneaker in the process. He didn't stop crawling until the tips of his claws—then his knuckles—then the top of his head—struck the wall. Then he curled up as small as he could in the tight space.

Somehow he knew—he could feel—the so-called maid walking between the two beds to squat next to the night-stand near his head. Her presence didn't burn in his mind like Jamie's did. Instead, he... just knew... from the vibrations he could sense through the floor, through the nerves of his cheeks and on his neck and chest, in spite of both the bedspread and the carpet.

"You can't stay under there forever, Room 8."

The painfully bright mental image of Jamie blazed near the door, her hand on the doorframe. She was a like a spot of white-hot heat in his mind. He couldn't see her, but he knew she was confused. He could almost feel the expression on her face.

"Roommate?" Jamie asked. Upset as well as confused. Hurt? "What are you saying?"

"I'm saying *Room 8*, lady, not roommate. But speaking of roommates," she added, aiming her voice under the bed at Ash again, "you all better get out from under there before Daddy gets back."

"Tell her to go away," Ash said. To the so-called maid. He couldn't say anything to Jamie. Not coherently. Not without shouting.

He felt Jamie take a step into the room, burning brighter—hotter—with each step. She stood at the foot of the bed, close enough to cause him to burst into flames too. He tried to pull himself into a smaller ball. The box spring pressed down on him, limiting his options.

"Ash?" Jamie said. Confusion still. And pain. But also some hope. "We have to talk. I... I thought you were dead."

"He's going to be dead," the so-called maid said, "or something a lot more painful, if he doesn't get his white ass out from under my bed." She punched the side of the mattress for emphasis.

Ash focused on the so-called maid's voice. "Tell her," he said. "Tell her to go away. She has to go away."

"I can't believe you're hiding under the bed, Room 8. Especially *my* bed. Your room's got a bed. You could be hiding under there."

"Please. Tell her to go away. I can't— She can't—"

"I can't go away, Ash," Jamie said. A note of disgust coloring the hope. "I have to... When I saw you, alive, I couldn't believe it. I thought you were dead, Ash. And then my father..."

Her voice faded as thunder chuckled in the distance.

"Tell her to go away," Ash said. "She has to go away."

"The police said you were there when my father... disappeared..." Ash felt the intensity of her presence ease, just a bit, as her focus shifted to her father. The emotional mix changed too. Then she was thinking of him again, focused on him, and Ash felt like his brain was melting.

"Ash?" Jamie said, her voice almost a whisper now.

"GO AWAY!" he screamed. His voice came out as a muffled roar, nothing like the thunder laughing at him again outside, but still loud enough to hurt his ears as much as it hurt his chest and throat.

"You better go, lady," the so-called maid said in the silence that followed. "I don't think he's going to come out from there so long as you're here, and I really need him to come out."

"Ash... ?" Jamie whispered again.

Ash's heavy breathing was making the dusty air in his cocoon warmer and warmer. He kept his jaws clamped together. He would not speak to her. He couldn't explain. He wouldn't ask her to understand. He wouldn't—couldn't—try to kill her if she would just—"GO NOW!"

He felt her take a step back, as if his words had pushed her. He felt her put a hand on the doorframe.

She stood there a few seconds. Ash wished he could comfort her. Take her in his arms, and—

"Go," he said, his voice only a whisper now through the tightness and pain in his throat. He didn't know if she could hear him.

He felt her almost say something, then felt her walk away.

He twisted suddenly, trying to bend at the waist, trying to crawl out and follow her—

"Not just yet, Room 8," the so-called maid said. "Sit tight. She's coming back."

Ash froze, the rough material of the bedspread pulled tight against his face. What had he been about to do? Why was she coming back?

"Here," Jamie said, burning bright just outside the door again. "Give this to him." Then she was walking away again.

He felt the diminishing vibrations of her footsteps as she crossed the parking lot, then the street, and climbed into her car. He heard the engine start with a roar.

He was so focused on his fading impressions of Jamie that he didn't realize the so-called maid had moved until he heard her close the door to Room 6.

"She's gone, Room 8. You're safe, I guess. From her, anyway." She kicked the box spring of the bed, making it shake. "Now get out."

Ash didn't move. His heart still pounded and his breathing still came in quick gasps. He kept every muscle in his body tensed, clenched, held. He wanted to be certain Jamie was gone. And that he wouldn't take off after her.

"Ollie ollie oxen free." The so-called maid kicked the box spring with each word.

He wanted to ask for another minute. Or ten. He wanted to apologize. His jaw, though, was still clenched.

"Come on, man," she said, kicking the box spring again. "What's Tony going to think if he comes to see what all the fuss was about, and finds you all under my bed?"

At the mention of the motel manager, thoughts of Jamie began to evaporate from Ash's mind, and the full implications of where he was and how he had arrived there washed over him. He felt the fabric of the bedspread on him like the straps that had held him fast on the night James Derouen had died. Suddenly the air in his cocoon was close and heavy. He couldn't breathe.

He tried to roll over, but the bed was too low. Claustrophobia hit him and he felt panic that he wouldn't be able to get from under the bed before he passed out. He frantically kicked and pushed.

He came out between the two beds, the top of his head scraping on the leg of the nightstand. He pushed himself to his knees, then pulled at the bedspread, trying to get his head clear, trying to breathe.

"Calm down, man. I don't want you to rip my bedspread. And keep it away from the candle! And don't throw it—"

Ash jerked the blanket off his head and threw it on the other bed.

"Damn it, Room 8," she said. She stepped between the beds next to him and snatched the bedspread off the rat's nest, then backed away again.

Ash managed to get to his feet without having to touch the rat's nest or lean over the three flames of the still-burning candle. He stood there, shaking, staring at his hands, which were normal hands again. The heavy air of the room was stinging his eyes and nose as he panted. He started to sit.

"You sit on my bed, Room 8, and it will cost you."

He stopped in midsit and straightened. He looked at the bed he hadn't sat on. The sheets had been pulled along with the bedspread, but were still mostly on the mattress. The two pillows were in the middle of the bed. At the foot of the bed, the so-called maid had made a big ball of the bedspread, which was now covered with dust bunnies and dead roaches. She threw it on the floor near the door.

"I can't believe you ripped my bedspread," she said.

"I'm sorry." He wanted to explain, but he had no idea how he would do that.

"I can't believe you crawled under my bed."

"I'm sorry. I—"

She held up her hand, palm facing him. "Stop. You just need to go." She opened the door and stood next to it. The rain had stopped. "Go."

"What did she give you—?"

She pulled a white card the size of a business card from the front pocket of her hooded sweatshirt. She held it toward Ash, then threw it out the door. The card fluttered to the wet sidewalk.

"Go."

Ash went, stopping only to pick up his sneaker. She closed the door behind him as he bent over to pick up the card. Then he retrieved the umbrella he had dropped and limped back to Room 8 while the heavy clouds overhead growled at him. Whatever humor had been there before, it was gone now.

4

ASH SAT ON the unmade bed in Room 8 and tried not to think about what was in his pocket. He had dropped his sneaker and umbrella by the door and kicked off his other sneaker before sitting down. He pulled his legs to his chest. He hugged himself to quell the trembling in his muscles, and to secure his hands.

He had been able to shove the card—Jamie's card—into his pocket before he saw what she had written. Beyond the first few numbers.

He distracted himself by thinking of his hands, but not looking at them, in case they betrayed him again. His hands had been his hands again—no claws, no scales—when he picked up the card he wasn't thinking about. But the way his nails dug into his forearms made him suspicious, and his scalp still tingled from ten possible wounds around his ears.

Trying not to think about his hands anymore, he stared at the white plastic bag with his clothes hanging from the doorknob.

He could still do this. He could still leave.

The rain had stopped. More importantly, Jamie wasn't outside his door anymore. She wasn't waiting for him. All he had to do was walk to the motel office, look in the phone directory for the address of the bus station, and come back here. Then he could take the umbrella and the plastic bag with his clothes and go...

Go where?

Not home. But to Bixby. He couldn't remember the specifics, but he knew there was almost nothing left for him in Bixby, Oklahoma. *Almost nothing*, though, was a lot more than he had left here in New Orleans. Bixby would, at least, be a new place to start from. A new place to leave.

He just had to get there.

And the first step was to leave his room—

The loud knock on his door caused him to jump.

"Open the door, Ash," Detective Marand said. The man's shadow darkened one side of the border of light that leaked around the drawn curtains. The detective rapped on the window with a knuckle, then knocked on the door again. "Open up. We need to talk."

Ash glanced at the glaring red numbers of the cheap alarm clock on the stand next to his bed. He had been going in circles in his own head for more than an hour. If he had just left immediately, he would probably have been at the bus station by now. Wherever it was. Or eaten lunch, at least. His hunger seemed to have arrived with the detective.

He unfolded himself and went to the door to open it. Detective Marand's distinctive odor of aftershave, coffee and sweat came in and wrapped itself around Ash before the rest of the man, still standing on the damp sidewalk outside the door, smirked and nodded in greeting.

The man's thick, graying mustache had been trimmed since the last time Ash had seen him. The matching eyebrows, though, over the gray-green eyes, were as shaggy as ever. The combination might have worked to make Detective Marand look less gruff and more friendly, but it didn't. Mostly, eyebrows and mustache added a sense of paternal disapproval.

"Aren't you going to invite me in?" the detective asked, with only the faintest hint of a *you-all* lurking behind the *you.*

Ash stepped back, opening the door wider. As he did, his stomach made a gurgling sound.

The detective glanced at him as he came into the room, then took in at the umbrella, discarded sneakers, and unmade bed. Ash made an effort not to look down at the bag of his clothes hanging from the doorknob. His right hand went to his pocket, as if to protect the card Jamie had given him, and the fingers of his left hand passed through his hair in an uncertain attempt at straightening it—and to see if he had drawn blood before. A quick glance at his fingers showed no blood.

"You hungry?" the detective asking, making Ash look at him again. "You had you some lunch yet?" When Ash shook his head, the detective nodded. "I thought as much. Pull your shoes on. There's a little place near here I love to go when I'm in the area."

Ash pulled on his shoes while the detective alternated between watching him and looking around the motel room. Ash wondered what the man expected to see.

It wasn't raining when he was ready, just cloudy, so Ash decided to leave his umbrella. He did pick it up and turn it over, though, so the drops caught that morning in the parking lot would drain. The detective watched him do that, as well, still without comment.

They drove away from the Tony & Cleo Motel in Detective Marand's dark green car. Ash noticed that "Tony" watching them from the motel office.

Ash said nothing, resisting the urge to ask if "Tony" had called the detective about Jamie's visit, or if "Tony" was a confidential informant.

As if making up for his silence in the motel room, Detective Marand started talking, though not about anything in particular. As he navigated the narrow streets, he nodded to some of the houses they drove past, mentioning robberies, "domestics," and homicides he had worked over the years. When they finally pulled into a tiny parking lot, he said, "This used to a little Cajun grandmother's diner. The world lost a more than a bit of its spice when she passed, God rest her soul."

The restaurant had been a house, originally, smaller than it was now. Ash had no knowledge of Gulf Coast architecture that he hadn't learned on a bus tour of "Old Homes of New Orleans"—and most of that information had been broken and rearranged in his head since then, due to death—but even he could see the house was old. It had to have been built in the first half of the previous century. And painted maybe twice since then.

"This is the original porch," Detective Marand said as he pulled open the screen door at the front. Ash had no trouble believing that. The wooden floor of the tiny porch creaked under their weight. Four mismatched cast iron table and chair sets had been crowded into the porch, half occupied, and a glass door opened into the main dining room.

The floor of the dining room had been covered with linoleum in a black-and-white checkerboard pattern sometime in the last decade, making the flooring the newest part of the restaurant Ash had yet seen. The tables and chairs in the dining room followed the same mismatched motif as those on the porch, but had a fraction of an inch more room between them. There were no empty tables in the dining room.

"One of her kids took over the place," the detective went on, "but they pulled out after Katrina. So a new family took over."

If the woman working the cash register was any indication, the new family had immigrated from India or Pakistan.

"What'll it be, love?" the woman asked in a raspy voice, forcing Ash to adjust his mental estimate of her country of origin half a world away to the United Kingdom.

Despite the woman's appearance and her accent, the old, glowing plastic menu over her head listed dishes that at least sounded Cajun. Jambalaya. Red beans and rice. Blackened chicken.

"Don't order off the menu," the detective said when he saw where Ash was looking. "That's just for the tourists who manage to find this place. Chicken curry," he said to the girl, who picked up a waitress pad and scribbled something on it. He looked at Ash. "You like Indian?"

Ash considered the question—and the implications that the detective hadn't bother to ask until now. "I don't know."

"Make that two chicken curries," the detective said.

"Would you like any naan bread?" she asked.

"Of course."

"Tea or coffee?"

"Coffee for me."

"Tea, please," Ash said, on the off chance his opinion mattered. "Iced tea," he added. Then, because he was still in New Orleans, "Sweet."

"Got it." The girl made a few more scribbles on her pad, then shouted something over her shoulder he couldn't understand. "You all take a seat," she said, somehow managing to sound both Southern and British at the same time. "We'll be out with your tea and coffee as soon as."

"This is a good time to come here," the detective said as he led Ash back to the porch. "During the lunch rush, the line backs up out the door."

The detective rambled on about the restaurant until their food arrived. Then he picked up his fork in his left hand, a round piece of naan bread with his right, looked at Ash and said, "I heard you had a visitor."

Even knowing the question was coming—the question had to be coming; the detective wouldn't have shown up when he did if he hadn't heard about—

"Jamie," Ash said. The sudden tensing in the muscles of his hands and arm almost made him drop his fork. He managed to hang onto the fork—and not reach into his pocket to retrieve Jamie's card.

"The lovely Miss Derouen," the detective said, speaking around his first bite. He swallowed, then scooped up more rice and chicken in its sauce. "How did that go? Is she doing well? Holding up under the stress of her father being missing?"

"Her—James Derouen is dead." Ash had lost track of how many times he had told the detective that.

The detective nodded as if he were listening. "We certainly found enough of his blood to make that a distinct possibility. It's the lack of a body that brings up questions."

Ash stared down at the thick, lumpy sauce of chicken and vegetables that had been poured over his rice, but he didn't see the food. He closed his eyes, then opened them again. It didn't help. He still saw—

The great head thrusting forward, the huge jaws snapping closed on James Derouen's head and chest before the man could even scream. Then a jerk, the great head pulling back, ripping the man in half. The warm rain of blood on Ash's face. Then another thrust forward and the rest of the man's body disappeared.

There had been no chewing. Only a toss of the head and a gulping swallow. So there would be no body found.

He had described all that to the detective before. Several times.

"You won't find a body," he said again.

"So you say," the detective replied, acknowledging that much.

Ash's stomach surprised him by not being put off the food on his plate. The grisly memory had no effect on his appetite. He stuffed his face, hardly tasting the food, chewing as long as possible before swallowing so he wouldn't have to say anything more about the death of James Derouen.

"So what did you two talk about?" Detective Marand asked after a minute. "You and Jamie? Any plans to get back together?"

Ash's hand, with fork and food, froze halfway to his mouth. Or tried to freeze. He tried to force the shaking to stop. He put the fork down, carefully.

"I told her to go away."

"I thought you two had something special."

"We did."

Ash had told the detective all about Jamie Derouen. Because he could remember everything about her. About how she had called him *Marcus* at first. How he had skirted the legal edges of stalking to find her after a chance encounter at the Krewes of Cleopatra parade.

To Ash, it was all still fresh. Barely a week since their last rendezvous. Only a month since he had first seen her.

"So what changed, Ash?"

Since the last time he had spoken to the detective? Nothing. He still needed Jamie Derouen. He still had to see her. He still had to—

He stopped. He clenched and unclenched his hands in front of him, over his plate. A tight fist, followed by spreading his fingers as wide as he could. He was aware of the detective watching him, judging him, but he didn't care. When he could fully extend his fingers and let them relax without them curling into claws—and when they didn't suddenly grow gray scales the way he knew they wanted—he picked up his fork again.

"What changed, Ash?" the detective asked again. "I thought you loved Jamie Derouen. More than life itself."

He did. He couldn't stop himself before he said, "I do."

"But?"

"But," Ash said, nodding in agreement with the conjunction. "I can't see her."

"Did you know she broke up with that other asshole? Oh, yes," Detective Marand added when Ash looked up. "She packed him up and sent back to wherever he would have gone missing from. She's free and clear, Ash. Hell," he said, leaning forward, "even her father's out of the way, at least for now. You should be over there right now, making your move. You should at least give her a call."

The card in Ash's pocket seemed to burst into flame. He dropped his fork, spilling rice over the top of the table, and pressed his hand against his thigh to put out the imaginary fire. "I want to leave."

"You haven't finished your lunch, Ash. Don't you like it?"

"Yes. I want to leave." Then he heard the detective's actual question. He paused to taste the food he had been chewing and swallowing. He noticed the warmth the spices were generating inside him. That helped him think more clearly, and relax. Some. His hand remained on his thigh. He could feel the corners of the card on his palm, through the denim.

"I like the food," he said. "It's... it's great. But that's not what I meant. I want to go. To get away. Out of... here.

Away," he said again, but managed not say *from New Orleans* or *from Jamie*. From what he might do to her if he didn't leave. Or she ever got too close.

Detective Marand shook his head. "Not an option. Not yet, anyway. Look, Ash, you might as well settle in. Get comfortable. Enjoy New Orleans. You're going to be here awhile." He paused. "I was going to ask you to arrange a meeting with the lovely Miss Derouen—"

"No," Ash said.

"I've got her new number," the detective said. "She had to change it when she broke up with the other guy. Turns out, he really was an asshole. You had him pegged right all along." He paused, as if he had just thought of something. "Say, do you want her new number—?"

"No!" Ash said, not quite shouting. His hand clenched, grabbing the card Jamie had given him. His fingernails nearly tore through the denim.. He felt the card bend and crumple in his grasp.

The detective held up his left hand in half-surrender. Beyond the detective, other patrons of the restaurant had turned to see what was happening.

"OK, OK," the detective said. "Calm your britches. I was having second thoughts about it, anyway, after all the fuss this morning."

Ash forced his hand to relax. He brought his hand up from his lap and picked up his fork again. "What did 'Tony' tell you?" he asked, trying to distract himself and the detective.

"Why do always you say his name like that? His name *is* Tony, or near enough. And who says Tony told me anything?"

The distraction failed. He was still thinking about—

"I won't see her," he said. "I won't see—" He swallowed, then forced himself to say her name. "Jamie." Her name still set off tremors in his mind, but his fork remained steady. "You can't make me. I won't cooperate. Any more than I already have."

The detective made a placating gesture. "Calm down, Ash, I said I was having second thoughts." He took a bite, then asked, "So did she say anything about her father?"

"She," Ash started. After a few seconds, he said, "She said... the police had told her... I was there. When her father..." He decided that was enough, and took a bite.

"That it?"

Ash nodded. "You could ask the maid, if you want. She was there."

"Was she?" the detective asked with poorly feigned surprise. "I will."

Ash scooped another forkful of rice and chicken into his mouth.

"So that's it?" the detective said. "That's all you talked about?"

"We didn't... talk," Ash said after chewing and swallowing. "She—Jamie—showed up. I... shouted at her to leave. To go away. And she left. That's it."

"She didn't give you anything?"

"No."

The detective made a noncommittal sound and resumed eating.

"That was it," Ash said again. The detective could learn the rest from the so-called maid. Assuming the man hadn't already talked to her.

The detective made another noncommittal grunt.

Ash stopped himself before he asked the detective where he could find the bus station.

5

THE DETECTIVE PULLED up in front of Room 8. He left the engine running as he took his phone from the pocket of his shirt and looked at the display.

"So I'll be by tomorrow and bring that Jazzy Pass," the detective told Ash and the phone.

Ash nodded, not because he believed the detective would actually let him roam New Orleans unsupervised but because some response seemed expected. And because he hoped it would hide his relief that the detective wouldn't be coming into his room and getting another chance to notice his preparations for leaving, such as they were. Still, he could feel the detective watching him askance.

He opened the car door and stepped out. He looked over the top of the car toward Room 6. The door to the so-called maid's room was closed. "Daddy's" brown and green patchwork of a sedan was parked out front.

"Looks like Daddy's home," Detective Marand said, as if he had read Ash's mind, "so I'll have my little chat with our favorite multidisciplinary maid, the Miss Makayla Byrd, at a later time."

34

No response seemed necessary to this, so Ash stepped away from the car and closed the door. He looked around but saw no sign of Jamie's red sports car. He didn't realize how scared he had been that she might have returned until he felt the relief from her not being there.

He didn't look back at the detective as he walked to his door, used his key to unlock it, and went inside. He considered not turning on the light because he didn't need it, then decided it would be better if the detective saw the light come on.

He was lying on his bed a minute later, staring at the nine numbers scrawled on the back of a business card for a boutique *parfumerie*, when he finally heard the detective's car back out of the parking spot and drive away.

He didn't remember taking the card Jamie had given him from his pocket.

The card smelled strongly of flowers and spices. Only the faintest hint of Jamie's scent lingered on the card, probably where her fingers had touched it. His own fingers had tried to press the card flat again, to remove the creases made in his pocket. His thumb kept rubbing over the numbers, smudging the ink.

He managed to push the card back into his pocket.

He sat up.

The plastic bag with his clothes swung like a cheap pendulum from the doorknob, ticking off the slow seconds since the detective's departure. He decided to wait at least an hour before going to the motel office. Just to be sure the detective was really gone. And to be certain he didn't get lost in the maze of his own mind again, or fall asleep from boredom, he set the alarm on the clock next to his bed. Then, as the silence of his room became deeper and he began to hear the voices and movements of the motel's other occupants through the walls, he turned on the TV and pushed the volume to what would otherwise be an uncomfortable level.

An hour wasn't enough time to run a bath and properly enjoy it, especially since his previous bath had been only a couple hours before, so he stayed on his bed. He didn't even kick off his sneakers. He lay on his back again, his arms spread wide to prevent him from taking the card from his pocket, and stared at the cracked and—somehow—stained ceiling, ignoring the car dealers and local newsbreaks and talk show hosts on the TV and the sounds of a shouted argument coming from Room 6. Or tried to ignore them.

He had heard the so-called maid and "Daddy" going at it before. Most of the arguments centered on her not giving him enough of the money she earned, or not caring for him properly or with sufficient gratitude. She was, Daddy was always certain, holding out on him. There had also been an argument about how she could earn more if she would charge more, and how she couldn't charge more if he didn't get off his lazy ass and clean his half of the room more than once a year. Room rates versus car rates, and so on.

Letting his mind drift, he tried to figure out if "Tony" was maybe short for Anton, since the motel manager *might* be Russian—or Iranian. Ash's fractured memories had left most of his formal education in shards, including all geography outside New Orleans. He didn't notice the argument behind the jabber of talk show hosts had changed tenor until he heard the first scream.

He sat up on his bed.

Behind the allegations of sexual misconduct being discussed over glasses of red wine on the TV screen, Daddy was shouting. The words were unintelligible. The anger was not. Ash could almost feel the heat of the man's rage on his face, as if the spiral burner on an electric stove had been left on, radiating a shimmering, tightly coiled red.

The words paused. Another scream, less loud, but with more pain. Less wounded outrage, more pleading.

Ash pushed himself free of the tangle of bedspread and sheets on his unmade bed as Daddy's shouts became a staccato beat of rage and the so-called maid's cries dwindled to a whimper.

He left his door open as he walked to the door of Room 6. The sky above the motel had lowered and darkened, but there was no rain. The heavy door of Room 6 was closed, but it did little to muffle Daddy's voice.

"Don't you tell me you didn't do nothing, you little bitch," Daddy was saying. "I got eyes, girl. I can see what's going on."

Ash pressed his hands against the metal door. He could *feel* the man on the other side winding himself up, preparing to strike again. Ash curled his right hand into a fist, then pounded on the door, hoping to interrupt the man's thoughts, stop the next blow.

Thunder rolled above the clouds in time with the knocks on the door, and the beat of Ash's heart.

There was no response from inside Room 6, just silence.

Ash glanced at the sky. If it started to rain again, he would get soaked. There was very little overhang from the roof, and he had left his umbrella in his room.

He focused on the door in front of him again. He pounded on the door, stirring up more thunder and a more imminent threat of rain.

"Who's there?"

Ash didn't answer, and stepped to one side so he wouldn't be clearly visible from the room's window.

"Don't you go nowhere. You stay right where you are."

Ash saw the curtain move from the side of his eye. From the other side, he thought he also saw "Tony" taking an interest, craning his neck from his stool in the motel office.

Ash pounded on the door again. He ignored the rumblings in the sky and focused on Daddy. He needed the man to open the door. He hoped the man wouldn't attack him, but he needed the door to open. So the so-called maid—Kayla—could escape.

"You mind your own business, whoever you are," Daddy said. "You go on your way."

Lightning flashed overhead as Ash hit the door again, three times, hard enough to sting.

"Open the door," he said in the lull before the crash of thunder.

The door opened as he drew back his fist to hit it again.

Daddy stood there in the rumpled, gray denim overalls he always seemed to wear. He wore a blue long sleeve tee-shirt under the overalls. From his face, Ash guessed the man was only a few years older than he was, late thirties or early forties. The man's bloodshot brown eyes were even with Ash's, but the other man was at least twenty pounds heavier. Fortunately, in Ash's opinion, most of the extra weight was rounding the man's face and pushing at the front of the overalls, not filling the chest and shoulders of the man's shirt.

Daddy flinched at the sight of Ash's raised fist, then stood straight again and tried to fill the entire doorway. "What the fuck you want?"

Ash brought his hand down, but didn't unclench it and he didn't step back. Daddy clenched his own fist in response. Ash noticed the red bruising on the knuckles.

Now that he was face to face with the man, Ash wondered what the next step was. What he should say. He couldn't remember if he had ever done this sort of thing. He didn't think so. Neither did his heart, which was pounding.

Movement in the shadows behind Daddy drew Ash's attention. Kayla, the so-called maid, lay huddled in a ball in the corner of the room, on the far side of the desk with the TV. She glared at Ash, as if he had interrupted her and Daddy's discussion. Which he had. The swelling of her left eye was clear, and blood trickled from the burst skin on her cheek below the eye. The left side of her lips were also bloody.

Daddy let go of the door with his left hand, letting it swing free as he stepped closer to Ash. "What the fuck are you looking at, asshole?"

Ash still didn't back away. His eyes met Daddy's.

Daddy made as if to move closer, but there was no more room. He leaned forward instead, so they stood nose to nose.

Ash felt his nostrils flare and saw Daddy's do the same. He smelled draft beer and rotting teeth on the man's breath, and some part of his brain collated the fresh smell of the man's sweat with what Ash had first smelled when he invaded Room 6 earlier. This was the rat who lived in the rat's nest.

"You came knocking on my door, asshole," Daddy said. "So what you want to talk about, huh?"

Ash's mind offered nothing useful to say to Daddy, so he spoke to Kayla. It still didn't feel right to use her name, though. He said, "Are you OK?" He didn't let his eyes leave those of Daddy.

"Yeah, man," Daddy said, tilting his head but keeping his eyes on Ash's, as well. "I'm great. I'm fine. I'm more than fucking OK. I'm the best I've ever been. Or I would be if my little girl here would give me my money." He brought up his right hand, and poked Ash in the shoulder with his index finger. "And if nosy motherfucking tourists like you would mind their own fucking business. How about you? Are you happy? Yeah? Now you get the fuck out of here."

Ash felt the man shift his weight, drawing his fist back, as Kayla said, "Daddy! No!"

Daddy stopped in midpunch, his fist six inches from Ash's left eye.

Ash stood still, unflinching, as if he had been willing to take the punch instead of completely unsure what he was supposed to do. Or how he was supposed to respond. Except for his racing heart, his body was acting far tougher and more nonchalant than seemed possible, given the circumstances. He felt goose bumps run down both his arms and his spine and hoped he hadn't just grown gray scales again. Though the claws might come in handy.

Daddy laughed, as if Ash's lack of response to almost being punched amused him, and he broke eye contact. He glanced back at Kayla, then looked at Ash again.

"You know what?" Daddy said. "I was leaving anyway." He turned his back on Ash and faced Kayla, who had managed to stand in the corner. She flinched, turning her face away as Daddy looked at her. "You know what this means, don't you, girl? Now you owe me twice. Twice," he said again as he bent over to pick up his wallet and keys off the floor near the foot of her bed. "I'll be back," he added, "and you're going to owe me twice."

Ash hadn't moved from the door, so Daddy stepped face to face with him again. Daddy's lips wore a lopsided smile, but his eyes were emotionless. He held himself warily, as if he still expected Ash to do something violent. "If you will excuse me, Mister Nosy Tourist."

Ash didn't respond for a long few seconds as his nose registered the smell of fear beneath the facade of bravado. He was still wondering what he would have done—what would have happened—if Daddy had actually carried through with the punch. And he wondered if he had ever smelled someone's fear before.

Ash stepped aside.

Daddy pushed past him, trying to push Ash out of the way with a shoulder. Somehow Ash's body had expected that, and he leaned back just enough so they never touched.

Ash turned to watch Daddy as the man went to his car door, pulled it open and got in. Scattered drops of rain fell and landed on the hood and windshield of the car. Daddy avoided making eye contact with Ash as he started the car, put it in reverse and backed away with the wipers going. Just before he drove away, though, he smiled at Ash and waved a middle finger.

Ash glanced at the motel's office in time to see "Tony" turning away.

The door to Room 6 almost him in the nose when he turned to check on Kayla. He caught the door just in time with his right hand.

"Go away, Room 8," Kayla said from the other side of the door. Her voice was thick with emotion and she sounded like she had a cold. She pushed against her side of the door.

"Ash," he said, pushing back just enough to keep the door from closing. "My name is Ash."

"You think I don't know that by now, Room 8?"

He kept his hand on the door. "Are you OK?"

"Oh, yeah, Room 8, I'm as peachy as a Georgia summer. You all just go back to your room—"

"Kayla—"

The door swung open and she stood there, jaw clenched, lips pressed together into a tight line that was twisted by the gash on the left side. Her left eye had swollen almost shut, but her right eye glared enough for both. "Don't you call me that," she said. "Only..." Her jaw trembled, and a drop of blood fell from her chin. She looked away. "Only Daddy calls me that." She met his eyes again. "My name is Makayla."

"Makayla—"

She started to shut the door again, but he caught it with his right hand again.

"Go back to your room, Room 8," she said. "This doesn't concern you."

"No," Ash said. "This does concern me. It concerns me a lot. I mean... I owe you. You helped me—earlier. I want to help you."

"What?" She shook her head. "I didn't help you. You all crawled under my bed and ruined my bedspread and the rest of my day. That is the opposite of me helping you."

Ash felt his face flush. "I'm sorry—"

Makayla sighed. "Don't be saying you're sorry again. Just... don't."

"Let me help you."

"How are you going to help me, Room 8? You all a doctor? Or maybe you got a first-aid kit hidden in your room somewhere?"

"No..."

"You don't even have a car, Room 8, so you can't even give me a lift to the emergency room."

"I could walk with you," Ash said. "To the emergency room. I have an umbrella." He paused, then added "If you know where it is. The emergency room, I mean."

She sighed again and looked tired. She leaned against the door. "You all got forty bucks?" she asked after a few seconds.

"Will that be enough for the emergency room?"

She managed a weak chuckle out of half her mouth and shook her head. "No, but it'll be enough to get Daddy off my back."

Ash took the small wad of bills out of his front pocket, along with the rumpled card with Jamie's phone number. He doubted sixty dollars was enough to get a bus ticket, anyway. He would just hitchhike his way out of town. As soon as he got a map. He picked out two rumpled twenty-dollar bills and handed them to her with his left hand while he forced his right hand to put the remainder—and the card with Jamie's phone number on it—back into his pocket.

Makayla opened the door just enough to take the money.

"You all go back to your room now."

"Aren't you going to the emergency room? Or something?"

"I'll make Daddy take me when he gets back."

"What?"

"You didn't think he was gone forever, did you?" She shook her head. "He'll be back, and he'll be fine when he gets back, Room 8. You all just ignore any further arguments you might hear, and everything will be fine."

"I don't understand."

The right side of her mouth curled up in a half smile. "You're sweet, Room 8." She started to close the door again. Ash still had his hand on the door, but he didn't push back.

"Wait," he said just before the door fully closed. Her right eye was all that was visible when he asked, "Why do you call him Daddy?"

"Because he's my daddy, Room 8, and I'm his darling baby girl."

As unsure how to respond to that as he had been to Daddy's aggression, Ash took his hand away and she closed the door.

When he returned to his room, the alarm on his clock was beeping. He turned it off.

6

IN THE LATE afternoon, in the bathtub with his knees up and his head beneath the surface of the warm water, Ash felt Daddy's car return. The water muffled the actual sounds he might have heard, assuming the sounds would have been audible over the TV he had left playing. But the vibrations of the car's engine passed through the broken asphalt, and his footsteps through the cracked sidewalk, and the slamming of the Room 6 door through the frame of the hotel. All those vibrations played through the water of his bath and across the liquid surface in tiny waves that Ash could, somehow, discern.

Ash didn't understand what was happening to him—to his eyes, his nose, his hands—his love for Jamie—

It was hard to understand anything in his life that bumped against his thoughts and memories—and his desperate need—of Jamie Derouen. Introspection was difficult when all trains of thoughts led him to the same confused destination.

If Ash had known, that night when Big Man and Sneer pulled him out of bed, that he was being sacrificed for Jamie, he might have considered his short life well spent. He couldn't remember many specifics of his life before Jamie, beyond an extreme antipathy toward—or from—his ex-wife. All he knew now was that Jamie had appeared and his life had begun again, mere weeks before it ended. If he had known he was saving her life, even if only temporarily, the same way she had saved his—

But he hadn't known. No one had told him.

Say 'hello' to the gators for-

Big Man's last words to a frightened, desperate Ash, interrupted by Sneer's bullet in the back of Ash's brain.

James Derouen had been planning to kill Ash again, after he came back. This second time, though, he had taken the time to explain what Ash's death was for. And to show that he understood Ash was a messenger.

Because James Rémy Derouen had promised his first child to the alligator god of the swamps. The god who had finally tired of James Derouen's stalling tactic of sacrificing his daughter's lovers—including Ash—in her stead.

Except Ash hadn't come back as a messenger. He had been bait, and a witness. James Derouen had taken the bait, and Ash had witnessed the alligator god taking James Derouen.

And, for reasons not explained to Ash, the alligator god had left the reconstituted Ashley Turner alive.

Ash had been confused when he first crawled out of the swamp. He hadn't known a year had passed. He had only known that he had to find Jamie. To find her and—

That had been part of his confusion. His madness.

After witnessing the alligator god's wrath, though, and spending a week with his new conflicting emotions and dark desires, Ash was pretty sure, even without explicit divine explanation, he had been left behind to see to the final collection of the debt James Rémy Derouen owed: the man's daughter, Jamie.

The compulsion to rise up from the tepid bathwater—to call her, to find her—prodded and poked around the edges of Ash's consciousness. He was never completely free of that compulsion. Even in his dreams, when he wasn't hunting in the bayou, he walked the streets of the French Quarter or along St. Charles Avenue, looking for Jamie among the golden dresses and headdresses of a never ending parade of Cleopatras.

Even Detective Marand wanted to use Ash to destroy Jamie. The detective wanted Ash to stay in New Orleans, to help the detective prove that Jamie was complicit in the deaths of the men she had dated and who had gone missing over the years. The detective would never believe the story of divine bargains and substitute sacrifices Ash could tell him.

If he hadn't seen the god himself, he wouldn't believe either.

But Ash still loved Jamie Derouen. He wouldn't help either the god or the law destroy her. Which was why he needed to leave New Orleans.

He had ridden this mental carousel many times in the past few days.

The difficulty was—besides his compulsion to find Jamie, which could only happen if he stayed in New Orleans—was that he didn't know where he would go. Not really. Nor what he would do when he got there, except spend all his time not coming back.

His old life—whatever it had been—was gone. His ex-wife—whoever she was—gone. His job—whatever it had been—gone. His new life—

Ash placed his right hand over his heart again, to feel the heartbeat and prove that he still lived. Even if he didn't understand how, or why—beyond the now-obvious.

A voice played in Ash's mind.

This doesn't have to be the end, Ashley—

A fragment of a conversation that felt recent, which meant it had happened over a year ago.

If you need anything, anything at all, Ash, just call—

A woman's voice. Older. Maternal. His mother's?

Your mother said you were a 'very bright boy.' Detective Marand had told him that, in their first interview.

When Ash tried to visualize his mother's face, there was nothing. No images, no smells. No sense memories at all.

—love you, Ash, and we want the best for—

The words sounded distorted as they came out of the void in his mind, starting slow and speeding up. As if they only emerged after fighting their way past the event horizon of a black hole.

His family thought he was dead, or at least missing. He was certain Detective Marand had not called his mother to tell her her son had come back.

Ash felt the vibrations stirred by the engine of Daddy's car. Felt the door of Room 6 close again. Felt the softer, lighter footsteps he knew belonged to Makayla, the so-called maid. Felt her get into Daddy's car. Felt them drive away.

As if that had been what he was waiting for—and it might have been—Ash rose out of the bathwater. His nostrils opened and he took in a long breath. He wiped the water from his face, then stood.

He had a phone call to make.

7

ASH PUT OFF making the call while he dried himself, then again as he pulled on his boxers, tee-shirt and jeans. He wasn't sure who he would calling, but it didn't seem proper, somehow, to call them while wet, or naked. He also made sure he had put the card with Jamie's phone number on it back into his pocket. That wasn't the call he intended to make.

The old-fashioned beige phone had sat on the small, particle board desk next to the room's equally old-fashioned TV the entire time Ash had been staying at the Tony & Cleo Motel, and he had scarcely noticed it. Neither had Makayla, it seemed, in her few visits to clean his room. A visible layer of dust covered the phone.

After he was dressed, he stood near the phone and stared at the white numbers on the old-fashioned gray pushbuttons for a long minute before reaching out to pick up the receiver.

He picked up the receiver with his right hand, then transferred it to his left, where the curved, bulky object seemed to want to go. He held the receiver awkwardly, reluctant to put it to his ear. It felt more like a blunt weapon than a communications device. How long had it been since he had used such a phone? Never in his current lifetime. Though in the past week, he had not used a more modern phone, either. Detective Marand had simply shaken his head the times Ash had asked to use the detective's phone.

Who are you going to call, Ash? the detective had asked.

Each time, Ash had almost said *Jamie,* because that was the only person he knew to call. But he didn't have her new number then. He had her new number now—

He pushed that thought aside. He had someone else to call now. Even if he couldn't remember her name.

The numbers on the pushbuttons, arranged in their three-by-four grid, waited for him with more patience than the dial tone he could hear through the speaker half of the receiver.

A faded, half-peeled sticker on the side of the phone provided instructions on how to call long distance, but that wasn't what had him stymied. Some remaining muscle memory could get him through dialing 9 to get out of motel's internal exchange, then 1 to call long distance, and another 9—

After that, his hand got stuck, hovering over the push-buttons as if immobilized. Or as if it wanted to dial some other number he was trying not to think about.

He went through the sequence three times, each time replacing the receiver on its cradle to abort the call.

He sat back on his bed and stared at the phone some more.

His room was silent. He had turned off the TV before he got dressed. He couldn't even hear any of the other motel occupants. There was nothing to distract him. It was just him and the phone.

His eyes locked on the 0 button. He could call the operator, ask for directory service in Bixby, Oklahoma, and ask for his mother's number. Could. If he knew her name. Or his father's name. He assumed they had the same last name, but their first names were lost in the box of broken window glass that was his memories. He wasn't even sure what he had called them growing up, or still called them as an adult. Mom? Mommy? Mum? Mother?

If you need anything, anything at all, Ash, just call—

He stood, walked to the phone, picked up the receiver with his left hand, and started punching buttons as fast as he could. 9, 1, 9, 1, 8, 5...

He hung up.

He picked up the receiver and started dialing the number he had memorized from Jamie's card. His left hand slammed down the receiver just before his right hand could punch the last button.

No.

He sat back on his bed, forcing himself to think about the person he could no longer remember.

—just call—

He stood, grabbed the receiver again and pushed buttons as fast as he could, trying to outrace his broken mind. After eleven buttons had been pushed, he stopped. He heard a series of clicks, followed by the purring sound of a ring on the far end of the line.

He resisted the urge to hang up. It was probably a wrong number. But he wouldn't know until someone answered. Maybe not even then.

He stood still, listening to each ring, hoping he would know what to say when the phone was answered. On the fifth ring, the call connected.

"Hello," said a man's voice. A voice so familiar Ash knew the man would be disappointed Ash had no idea who he was. "You have reached nine-one-eight..."

Ash stopped listening as the recorded voice recited the numbers he had just watched himself dial. He waited for the beep telling him he was being recorded.

"Hi," he said. His heart beat calmly in his chest, unflustered. His mind, however, was in turmoil. He didn't know where to begin. "Is this...? I'm... it's... this is... Ash—"

"Hello?" said a woman's voice. The same voice who had told him to *just call*. If he needed anything. *Anything at all.* "Who is this?"

"Who is it?" asked a man's voice in the background. The same voice from the message, with an irritation some part of Ash recognized and cringed to hear.

Ash took a deep breath and forced himself to be coherent. "It's Ash. Ashley."

"Ashley." The woman's voice had become a whisper.

"It's him again, isn't it?" asked the man's voice on the other end. Irritation had become anger. "Why do you keep answering?"

"Hello?" Ash said.

"You can't keep calling me," the woman said. She wasn't whispering any longer. Her voice was tight, controlled, but only just. "This has to stop."

"We're going to have to disconnect that line," the man said. "We don't need it, and I'm tired of this."

"Wait!" Ash said. "What—?"

"Good-bye," the woman said, and sobbed as she ended the call on the other end.

After a scratchy silence, the dial tone buzz-buzzed in his ear to reinforce his mother's good-bye. He knew who she was now, and that he called her *Mom*—he could almost remember her face—but the call was over.

He hung up, then dialed again.

This time the phone was answered immediately.

"Stop calling," the man's voice said, low, growling, angry and hurt and frustrated. He hung up immediately.

The third time Ash dialed the number, the call rang and rang. Dad?—surely not Mom?—one of them must have unplugged the old cordless-phone-plus-answering-machine from the wall. He could visualize the phone. His parents—Mom and Dad—had had the phone for years. Decades. Why could he remember the phone, but not their faces?

"There's no answer," said a recorded voice.

Ash put the receiver down on its cradle, interrupting whatever additional instructions the recorded voice tried to impart. He sat down on the bed again and stared at the phone.

Outside his room, the gray, overcast day had become night. The only light in his room came from the bright red numbers of the clock on the night stand behind him. His faint shadow on the wall was a dark Ash-shaped blot in a red field.

He noticed his heart was still beating normally. As if nothing had happened. His mind, though, seemed to be cutting itself trying to fish out memories and meanings from the box with his broken memories. Bits and pieces of memories superimposed themselves on his shadow. A man's face, frowning. A woman's eyes, crying. A hand touching him on the shoulder. A plate of roast beef with potatoes and carrots and a half-eaten dinner roll. His name, spoken with concern.

Ash...

He turned away from his shadow and his memories. And the useless phone.

To his left, his plastic bag of clothes hung from the doorknob, waiting for him. Unlike his parents, who no longer seemed to be waiting for him. Still, they were out there, wherever Bixby, Oklahoma, was. So he still had at least something of a destination, and a reason to go there.

He no longer needed to find the bus station, though. He couldn't afford a bus ticket to anywhere with the money left in his pocket. He could leave any time he wanted.

And he would leave.

Tomorrow morning. First thing. Before the detective came to talk to him. Before Jamie could come back or he could lose his nerve and call her—

He fell back on his unmade bed, clenching fistfuls of dingy sheets as he stared at the ceiling. In his chest, his heart finally started pounding.

8

MAYBE IT WAS because he hadn't eaten dinner after the failed phone call.

Maybe it was because the too-bright numbers of the alarm clock bathed the room in light the color of coagulated blood while he lay there waiting for morning.

Maybe it was because he heard muffled arguments and slamming doors in the early morning hours and did nothing. He didn't even turn on the TV to cover the voices and emotions. He just listened and did nothing.

Maybe it was punishment for running away from Jamie the previous morning. Hiding, when he should have been running to her—

He didn't remember falling asleep, but he remembered the dreams.

Dreams of swimming.

Dreams of waiting in the shallow waters.

Dreams of leaping out in ambush to catch an unwary deer by the throat.

Dreams of locking his jaws and tasting the warm, salty blood as he spun in place fast enough to snap bone.

Dreams of pulling the still-twitching carcass down into the dark waters of his home to eat later, after the meat had had a chance to rot properly, and marinate.

Ash woke with the tastes of rusted metal and decayed vegetation in his mouth.

Through his window he could see it was morning. Or close enough.

It was time to go.

9

LOOKING LIKE A tourist in his jeans and Mardi Gras tee-shirt, carrying a white plastic shopping bag and a folded black umbrella, Ash stepped out of Room 8 and pulled the door closed. He had considered leaving the room key, but decided that would tip off Detective Marand. So the key was in his pocket with the card Jamie had given him, plus the twenty, the five, and the four ones that comprised his "stash," the money that would, somehow, carry him... somewhere. Almost certainly not all the way home, but away from here.

The sun hadn't fully risen, so the west side of the Tony & Cleo Motel was a slanted pool of shadows. Only the windshield of Daddy's car was visible in the darkness, and it reflected the sky above with its scattered clouds. Maybe the sun would even come out today. There had been rain during the night, so there were beads of water on the wind-shield, and the air was fresh, almost spring-like, with a hint of sweet-smelling flowers Ash didn't recognize combining with the more chemical smell of perfume and the smoke of a cigarette being smoked nearby.

"You all checking out, Room 8?"

He hadn't realized he had heard the girl's breathing, and smelled her perfume and her cigarette, until she spoke. Her voice startled his mind, but his body had already known she was there, ears and nose tracking her.

Makayla squatted on the sidewalk next to the closed door of Room 6. She wore her oversized UNO sweatshirt pulled down over her legs and the hood up. She had her left arm wrapped around her knees while her right hand held a cigarette near her lips. The glowing ember at the end of the cigarette trembled. The flesh around her left eye was black and swollen in the dim light. The shiner was underscored by two bright white butterfly sutures on her cheek.

She turned her face away from his gaze.

"You all be good," she said, then coughed. "Don't be crawling under any more girls' beds." She chuckled at her one joke. "And get a manicure or something. You all did a number on that bedspread. Almost tore it to pieces."

Ash noticed a collection of fresh cigarette butts on the sidewalk by her feet. "You waiting for someone?"

She blew a cloud of smoke. She kept her faced turned away as she said, "You could say that."

He noticed the dampness on her head and shoulders. He took a step toward her. "Have you been out here all night?"

"You all need to go, Room 8, before you wake up Daddy and get his hopes up."

He took another step. He was standing next to the window of Room 7. "What's going on?"

"Just go," she said, still not looking at him. "No need for long good-byes."

The headlights of a car appeared on the street, cruising south. Makayla stood, tossing her hood back as she did so her hair fell loose around her face. Ash saw she was wearing the lace-up black sneaker wedges he had seen her wear before, and tight black shorts. The waistband of the sweatshirt dropped and covered the shorts so it looked as if she wore nothing else over her bare legs. She waved her hand with the cigarette as if to catch the attention of the car as it passed.

Her shoulders slumped as the car kept going, and she squatted again. She left the hood down.

He walked the rest of the way to her. She didn't look at him.

He didn't want to talk down at her, so he squatted next to her, bracing himself against the wall under the window of Room 6. He clutched his plastic bag of clothes and the umbrella in front of him. He didn't know what to do. He didn't know why he even wanted to help. If he was going to get away, this was his chance.

"Tony will be up soon," she said, as if she could read his mind as well as the detective. She still didn't turn to face him. She kept watching the street, her eyes moving side to side. She tipped her cigarette to shake off the ash that had accumulated. "Daddy too."

Tony might be a problem, but Ash could hear Daddy snoring through the wall behind him.

"Is he really your father?" he asked.

"You're not helping, Room 8." After another long drag and a cloud of smoke, she said, "If I told you he was, would you all think less of him? Or me?" She glanced at him, as if to gauge his reaction. Then she looked away again.

"And... this," Ash said, looking at the line of doors from Rooms 6 down to Room 1 of the Tony & Cleo Motel and at the street. "He makes you... do this?"

"He says I owe him." Her voice changed, taking on the lower tone and cadence of Daddy, as she said, "'For all those years of child support, Baby Girl.'" She laughed a short, harsh laugh. "As if he didn't miss four out of five. Or more."

"Why do you stay?"

"For the only reason that matters, Room 8," she said, turning to look at him. "Because I got nowhere else to go. Listen," she added, pointing at him with the cigarette, not waiting for him to respond. "Just listen. On the day I turned eighteen, my Momma met me at the door with a bag of my clothes just like yours. She told me I had to go stay with my Daddy now. It was his turn, she said." She took a drag on the cigarette, blew the smoke into the morning air. "I still had six months of high school, but she knew she wouldn't be seeing any more child support from him. So off I go. And here I am." Her right hand gestured to include Room 6, the Tony & Cleo Motel, everything. She turned away again.

After a minute, she dropped the cigarette butt. She made no move to snuff it. It just lay there on the sidewalk, the red ember fading into darkness until a thin steam of smoke appeared and was blown away by the morning breeze.

Ash didn't say anything. Like before, in the confrontation with Daddy, he had started something he had no idea how to finish. He had didn't know what he was supposed to do or say.

After a few minutes of silence, she said, "Don't you be feeling sorry for me, Room 8. I finished high school. I could show you my diploma, if you want."

As she talked, another car appeared and drove past. She ignored it, but a part of Ash's brain recognized the sound of the engine. It was the same car as before.

"I've even been taking college classes," she went on. "Signed up last fall. I've been... working... to pay my tuition. And our rent. That's why I'm the maid."

"Is that where you've been going in the mornings?" Ash asked. "To classes?"

She nodded, looking proud. "I am a fully registered nonresident student in good academic standing at the University of New Orleans." Then her expression fell and she sighed. "Not today, though. Daddy says I've got to make up for... for yesterday." She looked away.

"But he's the one—"

"Don't you worry about me, Room 8," she said, interrupting him. "I'll be OK. Daddy will calm down again in a couple days and our messed up little lives will get back to normal. You," she said before he could respond, "need to get a move on. Tony will be up soon."

Ash nodded.

The car came back for a third time, driving slower this time.

"You be good, Room 8," Makayla said and pushed herself to her feet. She pulled at the bottom of the hoodie so it covered her shorts, then started walking toward the car, which braked to wait for her. The driver's window rolled down with an electric whine. Just before she stepped from the parking lot to the street, she glanced back at Ash and smiled. Then she was leaning into the window, talking to the driver.

Ash stayed down, out of sight behind Daddy's car, until service and price had been negotiated—with a discount on account of the bruises and bandages requested and granted—and the car had driven away with Makayla in the passenger seat.

10

ASH'S MENTAL MAP of New Orleans before he died had comprised the French Quarter, the Garden District, and a handful of intersections along the route of the St. Charles Trolley. For no reason he could think of, most of that mental map remained intact. When he thought of them, though, he saw Jamie's face, which tended to derail other thoughts, rendering the mental map almost useless.

He had only the vaguest idea of where the Tony & Cleo Motel was in the New Orleans metro area. He was outside the normal tourist part of town. So he just stood, walked past Daddy's car, and walked along the street. Behind him, he heard the first stirrings of the motel's occupants. Someone opened a door. He didn't look back.

For the first few turns, he followed the scent of Makayla, which took him along the same route he walked to the sandwich shop. Then her scent faded into the exhaust fumes of dozens of other cars and trucks and the morning breath of their drivers as well as the toast and microwave oatmeal from the nearest houses.

He kept walking. When he came to the next intersection, he felt a mental tug to his right. He paused to consider his options, but left, right, or straight ahead meant nothing to him, and the cold morning air was slowing him down, mentally and physically. Having no other plan, he went right.

Within the neighborhood he walked and its narrow, crisscrossing streets, there were no signs beyond those identifying the street names. His only sense of direction came from the rising sun. He tried to keep it to his back as he walked. West, he was sure, was the only way out of New Orleans that didn't involve drowning in the Gulf of Mexico, the Mississippi River, or the waters of Lake Pontchartrain. He just hoped he would find a major street to follow before he found himself swimming.

He took another right turn and found himself squinting into the rising sun peeking over the sloped roof of a house.

Was he walking in circles?

He stopped and looked around.

The neighborhood here was a patchwork of architectural styles. Old frame houses with walls covered with honeysuckle and peeling paint stood next to much more recently built brick-faced houses with flat concrete circle drives. Old oaks and thick pines towered over transplanted maples with their tent-like support wires. Flat, empty lots were scattered throughout the neighborhood, some of them with visible foundation lines from the houses that had been there before and were long gone. Most of the lots sported realtor signs with phone numbers to call and web pages to visit. Some of the lots had sprouted pine saplings.

He stood on a fragment of sidewalk that bordered a cluster of empty lots that seemed to have been combined into one, larger misshapen green-and-gray Tetris block. He had no idea if he was farther from the Tony & Cleo Motel than he had been a few minutes before, or if he would find the motel just past the next corner.

He heard the sound of an idling car engine, and saw a car had pulled up behind what remained of a hedge row dividing the backyards of what had once been two separate lots. Twin tire tracks had been worn in the grass from the broken remains of a driveway near where he stood to the hedge that hid the car, showing that other cars had used the same parking spot. Further tracks led from the front of the car to another driveway on the next street.

The car rocked on its shocks as Ash looked at it.

The part of his mind that had begun to collect scents and sounds, categorizing them and collating them, told him this was the car Makayla had ridden away in. He hadn't seen enough of the car before to know, but he had heard the engine as it drove by the motel. He sniffed at the air and recognized the distinct tang of its exhaust and, beneath that, the scent of Makayla's perfume.

Ash let out a sigh. As cold as he felt, he was surprised he couldn't see his breath on the wind. Had he been subconsciously following the car and Makayla the whole time? Letting his nose and ears lead him along while his brain floated in a cold fog? Was he going to have to wait until the warm weather arrived with the spring before he could walk out of New Orleans?

He looked at the sun, then turned his back on it. West. He needed to head west.

Behind him, within the cabin of the car, Makayla shouted, "Hey now. Hey—"

That same part of his mind identified the next sound as one he had heard before, as well. The sound of a man's open hand slapping Makayla's face.

A red warmth bloomed in Ash's chest at the sound. His heart, which had been beating sluggishly, picked up its pace.

"OK, big boy," Makayla said, her voice placating, though Ash could hear the struggle to stay calm. He could also hear her fumbling at the car door. There was a click as all the doors of the car unlocked electrically. "OK. You all take it easy, OK? We're done here. I'll just let myself out—"

"I'm not done, bitch, get back here." The locks of the car clicked back into place. "As soon as I saw your face, I knew this was how you wanted it."

Ash's heart continued to beat faster and faster as he turned and walked toward the hedge. The warmth in his chest filled his torso and the hollow place in his stomach, reminding him that he had not eaten since lunch the day before. His nostrils flared and his hands stretched and flexed as he walked. He remembered dreams of hunting.

The car was parked on the far side, and the overgrown bushes blocked his view. He couldn't see inside the car, but he didn't need to see. He could hear and he could smell. He could *feel*.

The car's shocks shifted as the man moved. Another impact, an attempted slap but Makayla had blocked the blow with one arm.

"You all got the wrong idea, big boy. Only my Daddy gets to hit me—"

"I'm your daddy now, little girl."

Another blocked blow, but harder this time, and Makayla cried out.

Ash walked faster, spurred on by the beating of his heart and the hunger in his belly. The warmth spread through his shoulders to his arms, and poured down his hips and into his legs.

His mind flailed about, trying to think of what he could do as his body carried him forward, toward conflict. Would he be able to stare down Big Boy the way he had—unintentionally—stared down Daddy the day before? Or had things already gone too far for that? He didn't know and his memories were no help. He kept walking. Toward the fresh scent of blood—

Goose bumps that had nothing to do with the cold—and did nothing to dampen the heat still blooming inside him—erupted from the base of his neck and spread down his arms and his spine.

The bushes of the hedge were of some kind of privet with long, pointed leaves. The hedge had been left mostly to its own devices in the years since the houses had been removed from the lots. Ash dropped the plastic bag with his clothes and his umbrella and pushed through the bushes. He hardly felt the scraps of twigs and the sharp edges of the leaves on his bare arms and his face. He emerged beside the driver's door. The inside of the window had begun to steam.

He kept his left hand back and to his side and made a point of not looking at his right hand as he reached out to pull on the door handle. He focused on the shapes inside the car, especially the big one standing on its knees in the driver's seat with its back to him, its bare ass exposed, its pants and underwear bunched low, as it leaned and reached across to the other side. Ash pulled on the door handle, hard, his body expecting the door to open while his mind remembered the clicking of the locks only seconds ago. The door handle protested the mistreatment with a sound of cracking plastic, but didn't break.

"What the—?" Big Boy shouted as he twisted at the waist to see what was happening behind him. "Can't you see we're busy—?"

On the far side of the car, Makayla screamed. At the same time, she must have thumbed the button to unlock the car.

Ash felt the lock disengage through his grip on the door's handle. He pulled on the handle again. The door opened as the handle came off in his hand. At the same time, the door on the other side opened, pushed from the inside by Makayla.

Big Boy lunged after Makayla as she tried to scramble backward out the door, pulling with her hands and pushing and kicking with the heavy black sneakers she wore.

"Get back here, baby—"

Ash dropped the broken door handle as he stepped around the door. He bent over through the open door, ready to grab Big Boy from behind.

Big Boy's left elbow hit him in the face just above the left eye as his hands closed on the man's fleshy hips.

"Hands off, asshole—"

The blow staggered Ash and caused white flashes of pain, but he didn't lose his grip even as the man squirmed and pulled at his fingers with the other hand. Ash squeezed harder—hard enough he felt the man's skin breaking under the points of his fingernails, felt the first warm slipperiness of blood on his fingers—as he planted his feet, braced his shins against the frame of the car, and *pulled*.

"What the—"

The tone of the man's shouts shifted from surprise and anger to fear and pain as he was pulled back and away from Makayla, who fled out the other side.

Ash turned his face as he pulled the man close, pressing his cheek against the man's back. The man smelled of sweat and smoke and vinegar.

Once Makayla was out of the car on the other side, Ash shifted his hands and the direction of his efforts. He shoved

Big Boy forward, releasing the man so he sprawled across the gearshift and passenger seat, with his arms beneath him and his head hanging out the far side after bouncing off the interior panels of the dash.

Ash stepped back, straightened, and slammed the driver's door closed. He stared at the bloody fingerprints he left on the window and the door frame. Four smeared, red ovals with pointed tips spread wider than they should have been. His hand wasn't built like that. Nor was any other human hand.

He stopped himself before he lifted his right hand to lick his fingers, and pulled his eyes away from the fingerprints.

He stopped himself again before he wiped his hands on his shirt and jeans.

He kept his hands back and out to his sides so he wouldn't see them, and avoided looking at his reflection in the various windows as he walked around the car.

He failed to resist the urge to drag the fingernails of his left hand across the paint job of the rear door and fender, and left four bloody parallel lines. The screeching sound of the paint being scratched poked at his ears. The vibrations traveled up his arm like reverse goose flesh. He didn't want to enjoy either sensation, but he did. He felt his lips pulling back from his teeth as he smiled.

Big Boy had pushed himself to his hands and knees—hands in the passenger seat, knees in the driver seat, ass almost against the far window, dangling penis comparing unfavorably with the gearshift below him—when he looked up to see Ash smiling at him through the open passenger door. He jerked back and away, hitting his head on the interior roof of the cab, then fell against the far door.

Ash gripped the corner of the open passenger door and leaned over. He met Big Boy's eyes. The man's eyes were already wide. They went wider, showing white all the way around.

"What—what are you?"

"Hungry," Ash said, before he could stop himself. Because he *was* hungry. He had never been so hungry in his life. Hunger consumed him—

He spotted Makayla's tiny black shorts on the floorboard in front of the passenger seat. His smile fell away and he pushed his hunger to the side as he remembered why he was there.

On the far side of the car, Big Boy managed to open his door and fall out backward, much the way Makayla had on this side. He pulled his pants after him as he pushed through the bushes of the hedge and ran away. Ash let him go.

Ash released the door and fell to his knees beside the car. He panted, and the beating of his heart changed. His heart still pounded, but more like the after effects of physical exertion, not bloodlust. Still refusing to look at his hands, he drove his fingers into the dirt and grass, then pulled them out and wiped then clean on the ground by his knees.

When he held his hands up, they were just hands again. Dirt smudged his fingers and had caked under his fingernails, but his hands were just hands.

He ignored the smell of the man's blood that rose from the grass where he had wiped it.

He pushed himself to his feet, leaned into the car, and retrieved Makayla's shorts. She would be cold without those. He was already cold, the heat from before dissipating quickly.

He left the car door open as he turned to follow Makayla. He hadn't seen which way she ran off, but her perfume—and the smell of her—and her fear—hung in the air. He could follow her. She would know the way back to the motel, and maybe she could give him directions—draw him a map—for how to get out of the neighborhood. Out of the New Orleans.

The warmth in his body continued to leach away as he walked, and his pace—mentally and physically—slowed until he was plodding forward. He clenched Makayla's shorts in his right hand as delicately as he could. He didn't want to ruin them.

Ash didn't catch up with Makayla so much as almost walk over her. Some part of his mind realized she had heard him coming, then seen him, then stopped to wait for him. The other part of his mind had simply been following her scent and came to a stop when and where her scent stopped. Both parts of his mind then struggled to keep him from falling. He stood there, swaying slightly as he looked down at her, trying to remember why he had been following her.

She leaned against the corner of a wooden fence. She had been pressed against the far side of the corner, waiting for him to come around. She still smelled of fear and Big Boy's sweat and sex, but also of control. In spite of the cold, she almost glowed from the heat coming off her skin. She had exerted herself to run away from the car, then stopped here to rest. And... wait for him?

"You didn't have to do that," she said, standing and putting her face close to his. Her eyes glared and her tone was sharp. "I would have been OK."

The warmth of her breath was tangible in the cold air. He could almost see it. The sutures below her eye were still there, but the cut had reopened and blood leaked out. She had smudged the blood with a finger to keep it from dripping.

Ash eventually nodded and she stepped back. He stopped staring at the blood on her finger and tracked the engine of a car driving past on the other side of the road.

"If you all got hurt," she went on, "it's your own fault."

Ash shook his head. Unlike her, he hadn't run. He couldn't have. So he wasn't winded. He just... couldn't find his words in the cold, dark recesses of his mind. She seemed to be waiting for him to say something, though, so he forced out, "I... no. Fine."

"Me Makayla, you fine," she said in a lighter tone, mocking him. "I suppose that's just dirt on your face, is it? I saw him tag you with that elbow..."

Ash remembered the blow. He rubbed the side of his right fist against his face and winced at the tenderness.

"Well, now there is dirt on your face. How did your hands get so dirty? Did he kick your ass after I left? Oh." She paused. "Did you bring those for me?"

When he met her eyes again, she nodded to his right hand. He still clenched her black shorts in his fist. At the same time, he saw both his plastic bag of clothes and his umbrella were dangling from his left hand. He didn't remember pausing to retrieve those.

He pushed his right hand at Makayla and she caught it. Her fingers were warm, almost hot, as she pried open his fingers and took the shorts.

"Thanks," she said. "I think." She brushed at the dirt and shook them in the air in front of her. "You didn't have to do that, either. But, hey, you saved me five bucks."

A passing car honked as she bent over and pulled the shorts on. She pushed her feet through the leg holes, one after the other, without taking off her shoes. Then she turned away from both Ash and the street to hike up her sweatshirt, to pull the shorts into place, exposing her bare buttocks for an instant and earning a chorus of honk-honk-honks.

"How?" Ash asked as she adjusted her sweatshirt to cover the shorts and legs again. Talking required more effort than normal, but he managed to put the words together. "How do I get out?"

She sighed and put her hands in the front pockets of her hoodie. She looked past him, down the street where all the cars seemed to be headed. "I wish I knew, Room 8. I wish I knew."

"I got... lost."

She looked at him sideways. "So you all weren't following me?"

Ash looked back the way he had come. He didn't remember how many blocks he had walked from the car, or what turns he had made to get here. Then he looked at Makayla again.

"Not on purpose," he said. "The first time."

She pulled her hands out of her pocket. She held a cigarette in her right hand, and a plastic lighter in the other. She started to put the cigarette to her lips, then offered it to him.

He shook his head. He couldn't remember if he smoked, but he didn't think he did.

"You sure? You're looking a bit blue."

"Cold," he agreed, nodding. He crossed his arms over his chest, hugging himself. Then he shook his head again because she was still offering.

She shrugged and put the cigarette between her lips.

"Sun's up, but the temperature's down," she said, talking around the cigarette. She lit the cigarette with a long drag, then blew the smoke away.

She turned and started to walk away. She paused and looked back at him. "You all coming?"

He nodded, but didn't move. His legs didn't feel tired. He wasn't tired. He was just... cold. Slowly freezing in place.

She walked back and put her left hand on his right elbow. Her hand was hot on the exposed skin of his arm, but not painfully so.

"Come on —" She pulled her hand away, leaving a warm spot. She blew on her fingers, then touched him again tentatively. "You're freezing."

He nodded, slowly. He let her pull on his arm, disentangling it from his other arm. The touch of her hand helped. The warmth spread from her hand, up his arm and to his chest. His heart picked up the pace, though only a little.

He managed to shuffle forward when she tugged his arm.

"There you go. One foot in front of the other."

Each step was easier than the previous as her body heat transferred into him through her fingers.

"I'd loan you my hoodie," she said, walking in step beside him. "I probably owe you that much, but then I'd be freezing my naked little tits off more than I already am, so that ain't going to happen."

She moved her hand so it was in the crook of his elbow, resting on his biceps, as if she were walking beside him, her hand on his arm, instead of pulling him along. She was still the primary source of their forward motion, but it looked as if he were escorting her.

"I can't believe how cold you are," she said, taking a drag on her cigarette. "Once you're back in your room, you can take one of those long, hot baths of yours. Maybe there will be enough hot water left."

"How do you know... about that?" Talking was easier, now that they were moving.

"Tony told me. That man sees everything that goes on."

"That's not... can't be... his name..."

"Who cares? He answers to it. What else do you want from a name, Room 8?" She glanced at him. She might have been smiling, but it was hard to tell from the split on the left side of her mouth. He managed to smile in response.

She kept her hand on his arm as they walked since he tended to slow down or miss turns when she took her hand away. When she finished her cigarette, she tossed it into the street, then placed her right hand on top of her left, encircling his arm with her hands. The experience reminded him of slow walks in the French Quarter and Garden District with Jamie. Jamie had liked to put her hands on his arm the same way. Her fingers had been cool at first, but warmed in time. Makayla's hands were hot, though not as hot as they had been. He hoped he wasn't stealing all her warmth.

Makayla kept talking as they walked, so it shouldn't have been a surprise every time he glanced at her that she wasn't Jamie. But it was.

She met his eye when he glanced at her this time—how many times had there been?

"So?" she asked.

"What?" He had not been listening. He had been hearing her voice, but in his mind he had been hearing Jamie talking about a painting of a blue dog she wanted to buy. Not just a poster print, but the painting itself.

Makayla smirked. "That elbow to the forehead seems to have left you all a bit punch drunk. If either of us could afford it, or had a car, I would say you should go to the emergency room. You might have a concussion."

Ash shook his head. "No. Just... the cold."

"You sure? I thought I heard something rattling just now. Whatever. I thought you Yankees were used to the cold."

"I'm not... a Yankee."

"Anyway, why are you so anxious to get out of New Orleans? I mean, I know you're not from here, but why are you in such a hurry to leave?"

"I've... been here too long."

"There's no such thing. Not in New Orleans."

"There's nothing here for me," he lied.

"Uh huh. What about the pretty rich lady with the sports car?"

Ash clenched his jaw before he could say her name. His fingers twitched.

"Uh huh. I see. She didn't look that scary to me. You want me to kick her ass? I definitely owe you that much." She paused. "Or maybe we're even now."

Ash managed a tight smile.

"So where are you from?" she asked after another minute of silence. "How far out of town are you trying to go? Or get back to?"

"Oklahoma," he said. "Bixby."

"Never heard of it."

"It's near... it doesn't matter." After a second, he added, "I just can't seem to make any progress. I was going to take the bus, but I can't afford that now. So I was going to walk, but that didn't work either."

"How much money you got?"

"Not enough."

"*I* know it's not enough, I was just curious if *you* knew that."

"I have... some money."

"You got twenty bucks," she said. "Maybe twenty-five."

He looked at her.

"What?" she asked, meeting his gaze. "It's one of the few perks of being a maid. I get to paw through people's stuff. So long as I don't take anything, they can't complain."

"You took my change. And my bottle of cleaner."

"Nah. That was Tony. He was upset about all the hot water you were costing him. Anyway, how about you give me that last twenty-dollar bill you have in your pocket, and I will take you for a ride in my Daddy's car?"

"How far?"

"That's what I like about you, Room 8. Any other man would have thought I meant some other kind of ride. But, no, not that far. Not all the way Buttfuck, Oklahoma—"

"Bixby."

"Whatever. And I probably can't get you all the way to Baton Rouge, either. Not for twenty dollars."

Ash couldn't remember much about the geography of Louisiana, but he remembered driving almost halfway to Baton Rouge once before. He knew what was out there. "So you would drop me off in the swamp? In the middle of nowhere?"

She shrugged. They were walking close enough her shoulder rubbed against his arm. "You already had the brilliant plan of walking a million miles to BFOK and I didn't say anything about that, did I? This at least shaves off a bit and gets you started on the other side of the city line."

Before Ash could think of how to respond, she shook her head and sighed.

"No," she said. "You're right. That's a stupid plan. Almost as stupid as walking all the way from here to BFOK with twenty-five dollars and change."

"Twenty-nine dollars. Tony only took my change."

"Yeah, he's petty like that. Do you have family up there?"

He nodded. "Yes, but they think I'm dead. I tried to

call. It... didn't go well."

Her expression when she looked at him was odd. "Why do they think you're dead?"

He didn't meet her eye this time. "I was. Once."

"Are you sure you didn't get hit in the head harder than you think?"

He didn't tell her he had been shot in the head.

"Whatever," she said after a few seconds. "OK, so family is out. And I already know you don't have any friends—"

"I used to. I think. Have friends."

"What about the pretty rich lady with the sports car?"

"I—I can't—" The clenching muscles of his jaw chopped off his words.

"Calm down," she said. "I get it. She upsets you. But I'll bet she has more than twenty-nine bucks."

Ash tried to stop, but she pulled on his arm and kept him moving.

"I can't," he said. "Call her—" She might come to see him. And he would— "No."

"Fine," Makayla said, rolling her eyes. "I'll call her. I'll tell her I'm calling for you."

Ash stopped walking this time, forcing Makayla to stop, as well.

"I won't meet her."

"You won't have to," Makayla said. She patted him on the arm, then pulled until he started walking again. "I'll call her. For you. And then I'll meet with her," she added before Ash could protest again. "And I'll make sure she gives you cash. Enough cash for a bus ticket, at least. And some money for few Happy Meals on the way."

"And some for Daddy?"

She made a grunting sound that might have been a chuckle. "Not a lot, but some, yeah. Daddy will insist on payment for services rendered."

"You know… you don't have to do that."

"You helped me when I didn't need it," she said. "Only seems fair."

Ash had meant that she didn't have to give anything to Daddy, but decided to let it go. He just nodded, and they walked on.

This time it was her that pulled them to a stop. Ash looked around. They stood on the corner across from the Tony & Cleo Motel. The sky above them had cleared. No clouds remained, but even the morning sun couldn't remove the gray dinge that clung to the motel and to the cars parked in front of it. Daddy's car looked even worse than it normally did.

"You all better let me walk in alone," she said, taking her hands off his arm. "Daddy's already going to be upset I… I had to walk back. I don't want him to think you had anything to do with it."

Ash nodded. He felt warm. From the walk. From her hands. From her offer of help. Except for a lingering sense of panic at the thought of calling Jamie, he almost felt normal again. His stomach growled.

"You all go get some breakfast," she said. "But wash your hands first. And since we might be coming into money later today, maybe you buy me a Po Boy too. You can slip it to me when Daddy's not looking." She touched his shoulder, creating a new warm spot, and smiled a lopsided smile, as if she had just said something amusing that Ash hadn't caught. Then she stepped off the curb, walking diagonally across the intersection.

Ash watched to make sure she reached the other side, then turned to look back the way they had come. He wondered if the sandwich shop was open this early.

12

BUYING TWO LARGE sandwiches and a couple bags of potato chips used up nearly half Ash's remaining cash, but he didn't worry about it. Even if Makayla's idea didn't work out—he tried not to think of the specifics, so he wouldn't be distracted and forget what he was doing—he was sure he could get more money from Detective Marand. The detective wouldn't let him starve. At worst, the detective would cut him loose, leaving Ash broke and alone. Which didn't sound a lot different from his current situation. And he would definitely be free then to walk back to Oklahoma.

The rays of the midmorning sun offset the colder air as he walked to the Tony & Cleo Motel. Combined with the exercise from walking and his increasing hunger, it was sufficient stimulation to keep him thinking and moving deliberately, if slowly. He noticed a new line of clouds had formed along the southern horizon, reminding him that winter wasn't over, and that walking out of New Orleans would never be easy.

Daddy's car was still parked in its spot, but Makayla wasn't standing or squatting in front of Room 6 when he reached the motel, so he went into his room. He dropped his bag of clothes and the umbrella on the floor, turned up the heat on the window unit as he took off his sneakers, then sat on his bed. He ate half of one sandwich and one bag of chips while he waited for Makayla to return.

His eyes opened when he heard a light knocking on his door. He didn't move.

He lay on the bed, on his right side, his back to the bright indirect light shining around the perimeter of his window. He hadn't turned on the TV, so his room was silent.

Another knock on the door, louder this time.

"Are you in there, Room 8?" Makayla's voice, just over a whisper.

Ash rolled over, stood, and went to the door.

Makayla slipped in as he opened the door, her thin frame requiring only a few inches of clearance. She brought with her the intertwined smells of recently exhaled cigarette smoke and mouthwash. She was dressed the same as before, but her hair was pulled back from her face and held with a big, black clip that scraped against the door as she entered.

"Close it, close it!" she said, then turned and pushed the door closed for him. She stepped to the window, pulled the curtain aside just enough to see through, and leaned close to the glass, looking toward the motel office. She jerked her head back, causing the curtain to swing, then she met Ash's eyes and smiled. "I think I was able to get in before Tony saw me."

Her eyes swept the dark room and found the bag from the sandwich shop on his bed. She smiled. "Is that for me?" Then asked, "Why is it so dark in here? Were you asleep?"

She didn't wait for him to respond, or to turn on the light. She walked to his bed, leaned over at the waist and snagged the bag with her left hand. She reached in with her right hand and came out with the other half of his sandwich, which he had wrapped and put back in the bag.

"That's mine," he managed to say before she unwrapped it. Her smile faltered and she looked uncertain. "The other sandwich is yours," he said. "And the chips."

Her smile came back. "I knew I liked you, Room 8."

She handed him his sandwich when he stepped close enough, then retreated with the bag to the room's only chair. She sat with the bag on her lap, primly, with her knees and feet together.

After turning on the lamp next to his bed, Ash sat on the edge of the bed. He held his sandwich, watching her.

"This is good," she said, speaking around the first bite. "I usually grab something on the way to class, but... not today, obviously." She glanced around the room again as she chewed. She stopped chewing. "Didn't you put any hot sauce on it?"

"You weren't very specific in your order."

"Uh huh. I keep forgetting you're not from here, even though your fashion sense reminds me every time I look at you." She looked around the room again.

"There's chips in the bag."

"That's the opposite of what I'm looking for, but don't worry about it. I'll be more specific next time." She stopped talking to concentrate on the sandwich.

Ash unwrapped the rest of his sandwich and joined her. They ate in silence.

Something about the two of them eating in his motel room reminded Ash of... some fragment of a memory from his past. He thought of the failed phone call to his barely remembered home, perhaps because the memory involved an older woman, and an older man, impossibly old from the viewpoint of what had to be his childhood. The three of them eating sandwiches with soggy tomatoes and wilted lettuce while watching an unfamiliar TV show in a room with two beds in a place they had driven all day to reach.

Makayla said something and he focused on her again. She had finished half her sandwich, rewrapped the remainder, and put it away. She had taken out the bag of chips and opened it. She was looking at him as if she had just asked him a question.

"What?"

"Why do you keep your room this hot?"

"It helps me think."

She tilted her head to look at him as she placed a potato chip on her tongue. She crunched the chip, then said, "You all do look a bit more... present, I guess. Though you were looking way past me just then."

"I was thinking of... a memory, I guess. My parents, maybe?"

"I made you think of your parents?"

"I'm not sure."

"Your parents who think you're dead. I made you think of them."

Ash shrugged. "I don't remember much about them. Not really."

"I wish I could forget about my parents."

He went to take another bite of his sandwich, but his hands held only an empty paper wrapper, so he said, "Everything makes me think of something, but not a lot of it makes sense. Everything's... broken."

She considered that with another chip. "What happened to you?"

He crumpled the greasy wrapper into a greasy paper ball. "Didn't 'Tony' tell you?"

"He said you were a 'witness to an abduction.'" She said the last words in a fair imitation of "Tony's" Accent.

Ash nodded. "I was. But it wasn't an abduction."

"So what was it?"

"If Detective Marand hasn't seen fit to tell 'Tony' more than that, I guess he doesn't want everyone to know." He threw the wrapped into the trash can next to the chair where Makayla sat.

She noted the accuracy of his toss with a single nod of approval. "So what did you see?"

"I don't want to talk about it either."

She shrugged. "Suit yourself." She ate one more chip, then folded the bag closed and put it away with the remaining half of her sandwich. She put the bag with chips and sandwich on the floor next to her feet.

She stood just enough to reach the big, beige receiver, then picked up the whole phone and sat down with it in her lap. "So how do we want to do this? Any special instructions? Do you want to crawl under the bed now? Or wait until I have her on the phone?"

"I think I'll be OK," Ash said, leaning back and pushing his hands palm down on the bed as if bracing himself. "Here. I just have to... not think about... who we're calling."

"Who I'm calling, you mean." She picked up the receiver. It looked even larger and more awkward in her small hand. She held out her other hand. "Number, please."

Ash stretched out his leg so he could reach into his pocket. When his fingers touched the card, the thought of who had given him the card—and who they were about to call—and talk to—hit him like an electric jolt. His jaw clenched, as did the hand in his pocket, crumpling the card again.

"You all OK?" Makayla still had her hand out, but she had pulled it back some.

Ash jerked his hand out of his pocket, turning the pocket inside out and spilling the other contents on the bed. Dollar bills and coins fell on the rumpled sheets.

He thrust his fist toward Makayla.

She flinched, then recovered. She reached out her hand and put it under his.

He stared at his hand, failing to will it open, to drop the card.

Moving slowly, Makayla put the receiver back on the cradle, then put the phone on the seat next to her. She stood and stepped close to his hand. His fist hovered in the air near her stomach.

"Let me," she said.

Using her hands—her fingers were no longer hot, but still warm—she turned his fist over, then pried at his fingers. He didn't make any attempt to stop her, and all his attempts to help her, to unclench his fist, failed. Finally, though, she was able to free enough of the card to pull it out. As soon as the card was in her hand, his arm slumped to his side. Both of his hands grabbed handfuls of sheet.

She stood there holding the card, looking at him with her lips pressed together. After a few seconds, she asked, "What did she do to you, Room 8?"

Ash stared at the bent, smudged card in Makayla's hand. A few curls of Jamie's handwriting were visible. He managed to say, "Nothing."

Makayla made a mm-hmm sound then sat again. She smoothed the card with her thumb so she could read the number, then picked up the receiver and balanced it on her left shoulder.

"What's her name?"

"Jamie," he said, his teeth nearly chopping the word in half. "Jamie Derouen."

"OK, OK. Calm down. Wait. Derouen? Like the missing rich guy? Is that the abduction you witnessed?"

Ash looked away. "It's a long story."

Makayla made her mm-hmm sound again, then started dialing.

Ash turned back and watched her fingers push the buttons of the phone. The tension inside him built with each jab. He jumped to his feet as she hit the last number. His hands were still clenched, so he dragged most of the sheets off his bed as he did.

Makayla pulled back and looked up at him, her head tilted to the left as she held the phone on her shoulder.

"I'll wait in the bathroom," he said. He dropped the sheets and stepped woodenly away from her, toward the door of the bathroom.

"Hello," Makayla said behind him. "You all don't know me, but we met yesterday morning. You gave me your number—"

Ash froze, conflicting desire and fear tangling him. Holding him in place. He focused on the door to the bathroom, refusing to let go of the thought of refuge even as he refused to move away from the distant sound of Jamie's voice through the phone's receiver.

"Yes, yes, I remember you. Is Ash OK?" Ash thought he could hear sounds of a restaurant behind her, as if she had just sat down for lunch.

"I'm not so sure about 'OK,'" Makayla said, "but he's not hurt or anything. Well, except some guy tagged him this morning—"

"Put him on. I need to talk to him. Please. Put him on."

"I'm not so sure that's a good idea—"

"Put him on."

The paralysis holding Ash in place evaporated as fear overcame desire. He stumbled toward the bathroom. He fell against the doorframe. He looked back. Makayla held the phone's receiver toward him at arm's length. The expression on her face was a mix of irritation and bemusement.

She put the receiver back to her ear. "He just ran into the bathroom."

"Put him on the phone."

Ash turned away as she started to hold the phone out to him again. He fell forward, into the bathroom. He propped himself on the vanity as he grabbed the door and pushed it closed. Darkness surrounded him. The only light came from the gap around the door.

"Did you hear that? That was him locking himself in the bathroom."

Ash's eyes adjusted to the darkness faster than he expected. He pushed the thumb lock on the doorknob so Makayla wasn't lying for him. And to keep her—and Jamie—out.

He slumped down and pressed himself against the door. The wood of the door was cool against his cheek and his ear. He could still hear Jamie's voice, but no longer make out the words.

"No," Makayla said. "Don't hang up. He's here. I promise."

Ash heard the girl stand and walk to the bathroom door.

"He needs to talk to you. He's just... Hang on." Her knock on the door was loud in Ash's ear, but he didn't move. "Say something, Room 8."

"Jamie," he whispered.

"Louder, stupid. She has to hear you through the door, and this phone, which is older than my Daddy, I'm sure."

The thought of the door between him and Makayla—and Makayla between him and Jamie—Jamie only on the phone, not actually in reach, helped him relax. The conflict inside him ebbed. It didn't go away, not completely, but it dropped enough that he could think. He could speak.

"Jamie."

He heard the double-thump of Makayla putting the phone against the door.

"Jamie," he said again, louder this time. "It's me. It's... Marcus."

"Ash! Oh my god, it is you. What's going on? I thought you were dead. Why didn't you talk to me? Why haven't you called? My father—"

"Jamie! Wait, please. I can't... it's hard to talk."

"I can hardly hear you."

"I have to leave."

"What do you mean you have to leave?"

"I can't stay. Talk to Makayla. She'll tell you. What I need."

"Who is Makayla..." Her voice faded as Makayla pulled the phone away from the door.

"Hello, again," Makayla said. "Yes, my name is Makayla." After a second, she said, "I would put him on again if I could, but he really did lock himself in the bathroom." Another pause. "No, I don't know why. He just... gets like that when you're around. Or on the phone. You saw him yesterday, the same as me. Look, whatever weird relationship you all have is your business. I just offered to help him out because... because he's a nice guy... What he needs is money. To get out of New Orleans. He wants to get back to some place in Oklahoma. Where he's from, I guess... Buxby or Bufby or something. He just needs enough to get there."

Ash listened as Makayla asked for $500 and eventually settled for $400. Then she arranged for Jamie to drop off the cash that evening.

"No," Makayla said, "not *in* his room. Outside his room."

Ash felt the tremble return to his hands at the thought of Jamie being so close—

"She wants to talk to you," Makayla said, pushing the receiver against the door again.

"Ash? Are you there?"

Before he could stop it, his right hand slapped the door in front of his face. Then his fingernails gouged the thin layer of paint, as if his hand was trying to grab her voice.

Jamie cried out in surprise. "Ash! Are you OK?"

"I'm here," he managed to say. "I'm... I'm sorry."

"I don't know why you think you have to leave, but OK. Alright. But we have to talk before you leave. You have to talk to me."

"I'm not..."

"I'll see you at five."

He didn't hear the call end.

After a few seconds of silence he said, "She hung up."

On the other side of the bathroom door, he heard Makayla put the receiver back its cradle, then put the phone back on the desk next to the TV.

"You all got problems," she said as she picked up the bag with her leftovers.

Ash didn't respond. After a minute, he heard the girl let herself out.

13

ASH WAS STILL laying in the water of his afternoon bath, his head below the water, when he felt the door of his room open. He opened his eyes at the sound, but otherwise didn't move any more than he had for the past four hours.

The bathwater had been only marginally warm when he lay down in it, since he had insisted on filling the tub to capacity. The water had gone cold after the first hour, but he had remained in the water. He had more than half hoped he would drown, so he wouldn't have to face Jamie—and face his own conflicted thoughts and feelings about her—

Except he hadn't drowned. He couldn't remember if he had taken a breath before he went under the water. He wondered if he had slept, since time seemed to have passed more quickly than expected.

"You all in here, Room 8?" He heard Makayla's voice through the water. He heard and felt her close the door. "One of the other perks of being the maid. I have a copy of the master key."

He felt her footsteps on the carpet as she walked to the open door of the bathroom. He had left the door open so the overworked window unit could try to heat the water indirectly—it had failed—but laying in the tub as he was, he couldn't see the door.

Some part of him kept him still, waiting for the precise moment to spring the ambush. If he didn't move, the prey would come closer, and closer, until she was within easy reach of his teeth and claws. He could leap out, grab her and pull her under the water with him, spinning over to push her down—

Except even that part of him knew he wouldn't attack Makayla. It simply enjoyed the contemplation of the possibilities.

"Oh my god!"

The shout preceded the appearance of Makayla above him. She still wore her UNO sweatshirt and had her hair pulled back. She started to kneel, to reach into the water by his head, as if she were going to pull his head out. But she stopped as her brown eyes met his gray eyes. Rainbow sparkles refracted from the quantity of water between them.

He smiled at her through the water, showing her his teeth, and maybe hinting what could have happened if she had just leaned closer.

She scowled and slapped the top of the water, shattering his view of her face. "Damn you, Room 8. You all nearly gave me a heart attack."

14

THE SCRATCHY HOTEL towel wasn't going to be much use after Makayla threw it in the tub at him. Bubbles rose out of his mouth as he laughed. She stomped out of the room.

Still smiling, Ash stood in the calf-deep water and wrung the towel out as best he could. He flipped the lever to open the drain with his toes, then wrapped the wet towel around his waist and stepped out of the tub.

"Is she here?" he asked.

"Did I say she was here?"

"I guess not." He held his arms out at an angle and shook like a dog. Water flew everywhere.

"You're making a mess in there, aren't you? And you expect me to clean it, don't you?" Before he could respond that she was, in fact, the maid—or as he referred to her, "the maid"—she went on. "You know, Room 8, most white guys have to pay for me to see them naked."

He flicked his fingers, spraying off the last drops of water, then wiped his hair back from his face. "I thought you were getting paid."

"That is not what I mean, white boy."

Wearing the soggy towel, he walked out of the bathroom. She sat in the chair, her legs pulled up to her chest. She watched him as he made a pile of his clothes, then took them back to the bathroom. He dumped the clothes on a mostly dry corner of the vanity, let the towel fall back to the floor.

"So is that your plan?" she asked from the other room as he dressed. "You're going to lock yourself in the bathroom again?"

He ran his fingers through his hair like a comb. He still needed a haircut. "I'm not going to crawl under my bed, if that's what you mean. I don't even want to know what might be under there."

"You cleaned out under my bed pretty good."

He came back out of the bathroom and she looked him up and down. "You all really need some new clothes—" She stopped and peered at his face. "Your eye is looking... better."

His hand went to his face to touch his cheek beneath his left eye. He hadn't thought of his eye since he returned from the sandwich shop. He felt no tenderness in his cheek, not even when he pressed harder.

"In fact," she went on, "your eye looks fine." Her hand went to her own eye, with its dark swelling and stitches. She winced. "Hardly seems fair. White boys get all the luck."

He nodded. "I've been thinking that all week."

She scowled and looked away. "Shut up, Room 8, you all don't know anything."

He sat on the edge of the bed, facing her. The sheets he had pulled off the bed earlier were still on the floor, now with wet footprints. "What time is?"

She looked at him, then leaned to her right to look past him at the clock on the nightstand. "Almost five." She settled back in the chair. "Of course, you knew that right?

Because why would I show up all early? I thought you said this hot air helped you think?"

"It does. But when... she... is involved, thinking... gets hard again."

"Sounds like most men, to me."

Ash heard the powerful engine of a sports car pull into the parking lot of the Tony & Cleo Motel. He recognized the sound and closed his eyes.

"That's her, isn't it?"

He nodded. Then opened his eyes again. Makayla was looking at him.

"You all do have it bad, don't you?"

He nodded again. "Pretty bad." He didn't elaborate how bad.

She stood. She adjusted her sweatshirt so the hem hung past her shorts again, then reached up and removed the big clip. She pushed the clip into the front pocket of her sweatshirt, then used her fingers to fluff her hair. She caught him watching her and smiled at him. The black eye and split lip made the smile come out lopsided. Or maybe that was the way she had meant to smile. Either way, in spite of the growing tension created by the presence of Jamie outside his room, he smiled back.

She looked at the door, then took a deep breath. "Do what I do, Room 8. Just think about the money."

Then she walked to the door and opened it.

15

MAKAYLA OPENED THE door to his room enough for her to slip through, then quickly pulled it closed behind her. The sky outside had gone darker than Ash expected, but he hardly noticed the heavy black clouds that had rolled in, or the low sounds of thunder and the smell of nearby rain falling closer and closer. He saw only a narrow rectangle of the sloping red hood of the sports car and its near-black windshield. He heard only the sound of the car door opening. His intake of breath through his nose registered only the smell of Jamie's perfume and, below that, Jamie herself.

He didn't realize he had stood—or walked to the door—until he was pushing himself against the cold metal. He squeezed his eyes closed and turned his face so he wouldn't try to see her through the tiny peephole. He didn't need to see her to know she was there. And if he looked, he didn't know he wouldn't open the door and—

He tried not to think about that.

"Hello again," he heard Makayla said.

"Where is he?"

"He's in there. He's probably all pressed up against the door— Wait!"

Each of Jamie's knocks on his door sent a jolt through him.

"Ash! You can't just hide in there. We have to talk."

Behind her, Makayla said, "I don't think that's a good idea—"

Jamie knocked harder, louder. Ash trembled and shook with each blow. When the blows ceased, he opened his eyes to keep watch on his hands. To make sure they stayed where they were. To make sure they remained hands.

"Damn it, Ash. You can't just show up like that, then disappear again. Not again. I... I know what happened. Before. I thought you were dead. But now I know you're not dead. You found me again. I—" She stopped. "Damn it, Ash. Open this door and talk to me."

He heard tears in her voice. He had only seen her cry once, the night he was taken from her. For all that he loved her—and thought she loved him—he only then realized they hadn't known each long enough to have cried together. They hadn't even had a real first argument. The closest they had come had been when he found her again, the first time, when she was still calling him Marcus, and she had tried to send him away. To come back later. After Mardi Gras. And he had refused.

If he had listened. If he had gone away and come back after Mardi Gras. Everything would be different. She wouldn't have cried. He wouldn't have died.

Maybe they would have had a real first argument. Maybe they would have cried together then. Maybe he wouldn't have to wonder how much he loved her—for himself, for real—and how much of what seemed like love was the curse of the god who had sent him back to find her. To bring her.

He felt Jamie lean against the door on the other side. Felt her hands and her forehead pressing against the door in almost a mirror reflection of his own pose.

"You don't have to worry about my father anymore," she said. "He's... gone, and I don't think he's coming back. I'm free, I think. I want to... You're free too."

Ash grimaced and shook his head, grinding his forehead against the door. She might be free. He wasn't.

"Yes, you are," Jamie said as if she had seen him. "Whatever it was Papa was into..." She pronounced *Papa* in the French way. "Whatever he was doing... it's over now."

Ash continued to shake his head while she talked, but he couldn't make his words work.

"If you... if you have to go, Ash, I will understand. But not like this. Never like this." She paused. "I can feel you. I can feel you, even through this door. What does that mean?"

Ash didn't want to think about what that might mean. He wanted to think Jamie was free, and could be safe if he left. And she would stay safe so long as he stayed away from her.

In the infinite distance, beyond his searing bright awareness of Jamie on the other side of the door, Ash heard a low rumble of thunder. Then he heard a door open and close.

Jamie started talking again. "You came back, Ash. That's never happened before. I knew you were different, but I didn't know... how. And Papa wouldn't listen. Then... you came back, and Papa disappeared, and I knew, finally, everything had changed—"

"Daddy! Wait! No!"

"So I hear you all are giving away free money," Daddy said.

In his mind it was as if Daddy's presence wrapped itself around Jamie's, blocking some of her light. Letting Ash finally speak.

"Let her go—"

"Daddy—"

"You all stay right where you are. You too, Kayla. Ain't nobody going to get hurt, if everyone just does what they're told."

Daddy's voice was low, with a friendly, singsong cadence that was almost soothing. But Ash could feel the cold, hard edge of the knife the man held in his right hand and pressed against Jamie's neck.

Ash opened his eyes and turned his head so he could look out the peephole. The peephole showed him a distorted version of what he already knew. Daddy stood behind Jamie, both arms around her, left arm low, hand pressed against her stomach and pinning her left arm to her side, right arm high, the hand holding the four-inch steel blade of a knife against her throat. He had his head next to hers, almost cheek to cheek, talking into her left ear.

Jamie looked more startled than afraid. She wore a dark trench coat buttoned all the way up and belted across her waist. She had her hair loose. She tried to twist her head around to look at Daddy, but he stopped her.

"Let go of me," she said, her voice even. "You all can rob me without all the groping intimacy."

Daddy smiled. He wore a wellborn leather jacket over his coveralls. "But it's so much more fun this way." The fingers of his left hand grabbed at the material of her trench coat and he made a kissing sound in her ear.

Ash's hands slid down the door. His fingernails scraped on the paint, but they were just fingernails, not claws. His left hand found the doorknob and wrapped around it.

Daddy's eyes went to the peephole, as if he could see Ash through the tiny lens. "You all just stay in your motel room, unless you want your pretty rich lady friend here to get hurt. Like I said, ain't nobody got to get hurt tonight."

Ash's hand tightened on the doorknob, but didn't turn it. If he opened the door, he wasn't sure which one—Jamie or Daddy—he would be lunging for.

"Careful, careful."

Jamie's head pulled back as the edge of the knife touched her skin.

Ash didn't release his grip, but he didn't turn the knob either. His hand was caught in the same quandary that paralyzed his thoughts.

After a few breaths of stillness, Daddy said, "OK, now that everybody's calm, we can get on with this. Just hand over the money—"

"Daddy, it's only four hundred dollars—"

Daddy jerked his head to look back at Makayla. Jamie gasped in fear and pain as the edge of the knife drew a short, thin line of blood.

Ash watched the tiny drops of blood form on Jamie's skin. His hand started slowly turning the knob.

"Four hundred, is it?" Daddy said over his shoulder. "Four? That's not what you told me before, little girl. You and I are going to have another little talk about this later. About you lying to your daddy."

He turned back to Jamie. The knob in Ash's hand hadn't finished a full revolution. He didn't know if he had turned it enough to open the door, but he stopped.

"Now, pretty rich lady, you take out your designer purse or your leather handbag or whatever it is you got that money in, real slow—"

"You should listen to her," Jamie said. Her voice was still calm, but her eyes were wider and she was breathing in short, shallow breaths. "It's not worth it, robbing me in front of witnesses."

Daddy smiled. "Ain't no witnesses here, pretty rich lady. Just you and me and my own darling baby girl." His eyes glanced in Makayla's direction, but he didn't turn his head this time. "And my little girl always says and does whatever her daddy tells her. Eventually. Nobody else here, not even our man Tony over there in the office, is going to see or hear anything. Or do you mean this tourist hiding on the other side of his locked motel room door?" Daddy laughed. "Ain't no policeman going to try and make a case out of that. Not for a couple hundred— Not for *four* hundred dollars."

The muscles in Ash's arms knotted from the conflicting urges to hold the door closed and jerk it open.

"This isn't just robbery," Jamie said. "Or even assault. It's assault with a deadly weapon—" She stopped with a gasp as the knife touched her again.

"This doesn't have to be assault, pretty rich lady. Just hand over the money and we can all go about our evenings."

"I don't have the money on me," Jamie said. She swallowed, then licked her lips. "It's in my car."

Daddy chuckled into her ear. "That money ain't in your car. We're not talking more than a few bills, even if you took it out of the bank in all twenties. Like my little girl said, it's just four hundred dollars."

Makayla stepped next to Jamie's car and put her had on the latch. She pulled open the door as she said, "Maybe I should check the car anyway—?"

Daddy turned his head slightly. "Damn it, Kayla, you all will do what I tell you—"

Goose bumps ran down Ash's spine and his arms as he twisted the knob the remaining fraction of a revolution. A tingling, like a million needles, started on his forehead, then exploded across his face and down his chest as he pulled the door open. He felt the bones and muscles of his face stretching and warping and felt his teeth bulging against the inside of his cheeks as he stepped back and to the side, out of the way of the door. The door slammed against its rubber doorstop as his vision doubled and divided.

The door hit him in the shoulder as he stepped forward again into the space it had passed through an instant before. He hardly felt the impact. He was staring at the double line where the carpet ended and the broken concrete of the sidewalk began. It was the line he couldn't cross. He wouldn't cross. He didn't dare step outside of his room. Not with Jamie right there. Fortunately, he didn't have to.

Jamie's eyes went wider at the sight of him and her mouth fell open as he leaned forward and reached across the space between them. His mouth opened too. Wider than it ever should have.

Daddy was still turning back toward him when Ash's left hand—fully a claw—closed on—and wrapped around—and twisted—the hand that held the knife. Bones ground together and tendons stretched. Ash's right claw grabbed Daddy's left shoulder at the same time, and he pulled both Daddy and Jamie back into his motel room.

16

MAKAYLA SCREAMED AND Daddy shouted, "What the hell—?"

Whatever Jamie might have been about to say or shout or scream was lost in a grunt and gasp of pain as she fell forward to the floor and Ash dragged Daddy across the top of her. Daddy's right hand still held the knife, but Ash had twisted the man's right arm to the side, then yanked it behind the man's back as he first pulled Daddy past Jamie, then pushed the man back, further into the motel room. He heaved Daddy at the wall next to the door to the bathroom, then turned to look at Jamie.

She had fallen to her hands and knees just inside the door. He was next to her, standing over her, in an instant, and his scaled, clawed hands were reaching down for her before he knew what he was doing, but not before she had seen him for what he was becoming.

He grabbed her by her shoulders and with a force of will that nearly pulled his arms out of their shoulder sockets, threw her backward, out the door, toward the red hood of her sports car.

His body would have followed her—he *tried* to follow her—but his claws caught the doorframe and held on, stopping him. His left claw grabbed the frame next to the chain latch and his right hand grabbed the frame over his head. His legs pushed and his throat growled, but he didn't let go. A roar of frustration tore out of his lungs and through his wide-open mouth.

Jamie, her eyes on him the entire time, scrambled backward, over the hood and up the black windshield. He smelled her fear and wanted to chase after her.

His grip on the doorframe tightened. He felt his claws penetrating the plaster. The long claws of his thumbs dented the metal frame.

Seeing his struggle, Jamie stopped trying to run away. She sat on the cab of the car, staring at him, panting. Her eyes were huge, and the fear was obvious. But beneath the fear was a look of what might have been... understanding?

Ash tore his gaze from Jamie and saw Makayla standing behind the open door of Jamie's car. Makayla also stared at him, her eyes wide, her mouth open.

Ash wanted to tell Makayla that he wasn't a threat to her. That he needed her. To do the things he couldn't do. To talk to Jamie. To tell him not to kill her Daddy. But all he managed to do was roar again, and she flinched and cowered behind the car door.

Ash flexed his arms and pushed himself back inside his room. He slammed the door closed, shutting out both Jamie and Makayla. Shutting himself in.

After a few panting seconds, he turned around.

He breathed hot, damp breaths as he stared at Daddy, first with his left eye, then his right. He found it hard to look at the man with both eyes. But he couldn't take either eye off the pulsing of the jugular vein on the man's neck.

Daddy slumped against the back wall of the room, cradling his right arm against his heaving chest, his eyes wide as he stared back at Ash. His terrified, confused expression reminded Ash of Big Boy, back in the car by the hedge. The smell of the man's fear permeated the air of the room, a pheromonal beacon in the near darkness, calling Ash forward.

Ash stayed where he was. His claws opened and closed with the urge to feel blood. His tongue moved against the inside of his curved, sharp teeth, anticipating the taste. But he didn't move. This time it was his legs and feet that kept him back.

His gaze shifted from Daddy's pulse to the knife that lay on the floor near Daddy's booted feet. The polished grip gleamed and almost glowed in the darkness. Carved bone. Alligator bone.

Daddy's foot shifted, and Ash looked at the man again.

Daddy pushed himself into a sitting position, but didn't make any attempt to stand. "What the hell is wrong with you, man?"

Ash didn't answer. He doubted the man could see him in the near darkness.

"All I wanted was the money. That's all. This didn't concern you at all." As he talked, Daddy's left hand felt around on the floor near him.

Ash growled, a low sound, barely audible, but with enough force to rattle the windows.

Daddy's left hand paused in its search, and his eyes glanced at the deeper darkness of the bathroom door near him. "What the hell, man? Talk to me. We can talk this out. You and me." He twisted to feel on the floor to his right.

Ash took a step forward. He looked at Daddy with his left eye, then his right, moving his head slowly back and forth.

"You like Kayla, right? I know you like Kayla. Who wouldn't, right? She's prettier than her mother ever was, and shaping up to be a right fine piece any father could be proud of."

Ash growled again as he squatted. He picked up the knife. The bone handle was warm against his palm, but his hands were the wrong shape to hold it properly.

"You want Kayla? I can send her over here. Anytime. You just say the word—"

Ash tossed the knife, hilt first, so it hit man in the chest.

"Jesus—!" Daddy shouted. The knife fell to the floor as he jumped backward and pushed himself up the wall. "What was that, man?" He slid back down, squatting, feeling with his left hand again.

Ash watched, still crouched, waiting for the instant when the man's hand closed over the hilt of the knife—

Someone pounded on the door behind him. "Don't you kill my daddy, Room 8."

"You all just wait out there, Kayla," Daddy said, not shouting, but raising his voice. He had the knife in his left hand, blade forward, and he was braced against the wall. "We're talking it out, man to man."

More pounding. "Daddy!"

Daddy pushed himself to his feet. "I told you to wait out there, girl."

Daddy rushed Ash then. Daddy's eyes must have adapted to the dark, since he came low, as if he knew Ash were crouching. Ash rose to meet the man halfway.

Ash felt the steel blade on his ribs, just below his right arm. He brought his right arm up, catching Daddy's left arm in a lock, wrist pinned with his armpit, his claws sinking into the man's forearm. Despite Daddy's extra weight, the man's soft chest and gut bounced off Ash and he pushed the man back to the wall. The man slammed against it. Daddy's breath came out in a gasp. Ash flexed his arm, putting more stress on the man's left elbow and wrist. He heard the knife fall to the floor again behind him. He kicked it away with his right foot. The bone and metal clattered across the tiled floor of the bathroom.

Daddy squirmed, but Ash pressed him against the wall. Ash turned his head so he could peer into the man's eyes with his right eye.

"Leave," Ash said, his voice lower than he had ever heard it.

"I was trying to leave man, but you got in the way—"

"Leave New Orleans."

"We can't leave here, man, this is the only home me and my girl have ever known—"

"No. Just you. Leave."

Behind him, Ash heard the clatter of a key ring, then the sound of a key being pushed into the lock.

"I'm not leaving without my little girl."

Ash turned to face the man directly. He had to pull his head back to do it. Daddy turned his face away. Ash leaned forward until his nose was against the man's cheek. He blew out a hot breath, then curled his lips to expose his teeth. Daddy tried to pull back further, but there was no more room.

"Yes," Ash said, growling the word into Daddy's ear. "You are."

Daddy trembled and Ash could feel the warmth of the man's blood. He opened his mouth—

The door to the motel room slammed open for the second time that night.

"Daddy!"

"Ash!"

17

VERY LITTLE LIGHT came through the open door, but Ash felt exposed.

He pulled away from Daddy, letting the man slump to the floor as he ducked into the darkness of the bathroom and shut the door. He didn't want to be seen as he was. Not again.

"Daddy!" Makayla said. Ash heard her run to the man. "Are you alright?"

"Get off me, girl," the man said. "Get off me. Leave me alone."

"Ash?" Jamie's voice hooked Ash and pulled him against the wooden door of the bathroom.

He heard Daddy trying to get to his feet. "Damn it, Kayla, leave me alone—"

"GO!" Ash roared.

He listened as Daddy limped around Jamie and out of the motel room, followed by Makayla. He wanted to tell Makayla she could stay, but with Jamie so close he was finding words hard again.

Jamie didn't go.

The hollow wooden bathroom door was nowhere near as solid as the metal door to the motel room. He could hear her breathing. He could hear her heart. He could almost see her bright brilliance through the wood.

"Go," he said. Not a roar this time, but still loud.

"No," Jamie said. "You're not *my* daddy, Ash." After a few seconds, she went on. "I get it now. I think. Somehow, you're involved now, with the... the same thing as Papa. The same... whatever it is. Or was, now that Papa is gone."

"You have to go." He tried to say it softly, but the low tones still shook the door.

"I get it. You think you're protecting me from Papa—"

"No. Not him. He's dead."

"But I'm— What do you mean he's dead?"

"I saw him. Die."

In the silence, he felt her and heard her come closer. She touched the door with one hand.

He trembled. He wanted to tell her he loved her. That he was protecting her. From him. But her grief overwhelmed him. He smelled the salt of her tears.

"How—? No."

Ash wanted to comfort her. He want to pull her to him—

"I'm," he managed to say. "Sorry."

He heard her gasp, then choke back a sob.

"I'll... I will... leave the money," she said, her voice tight. "On the bed."

She took her hand back and the wooden door went cold against Ash's skin.

Ash listened to her leave, closing the door to his room behind him, sealing him in double darkness.

18

ASH DIDN'T OPEN the bathroom door until he heard her car drive away. He left Daddy's alligator bone knife on the floor of the bathroom. Maybe the roaches would find a use for it.

That he had been able to face Jamie—to see her, face to face, however briefly—to have her in arms reach—and not kill her—or try to drag her under and drown her—gave him something to focus on. He could think clearly, even if only for a few minutes. He would use that clarity, those minutes, to put as much distance between her and him as he could. Then he would never be a threat to her again. He could protect her that much, at least.

Lightning flashed around the drawn curtains, and thunder crashed immediately, shaking the frame structure of the hotel and reminding Ash of what it had been like to be shot in the back of the head. Rain fell hard in the wake of the thunder.

He picked up the crumpled envelope Jamie had left on the unmade bed, then grabbed his white plastic bag of clothes and his collapsible black umbrella. When he stepped outside, he pushed the spring-loaded button that made the umbrella expand. Between the umbrella and overhang of the roof, he remained dry from the waist up. Water started pooling on the sidewalk as he walked toward the motel office.

"I ain't leaving," Makayla was shouting as he passed Room 6. Ash could hardly hear her over the sound of the rain and the continuous rumble of the thunder overhead. "I have classes until May."

"You all are coming with me, little girl."

"No, I ain't."

Since there was only shouting, Ash kept walking.

"Tony" still sat behind the counter on his tall stool. The man looked away from the 5:30 news on the TV hanging from the ceiling in the corner to watch Ash enter and start shaking the rain off the umbrella and struggle with the release to make the umbrella fold up again.

"You are checking out? Yes?"

Ash wrestled the umbrella back into damp dead spider mode and dropped it on the linoleum floor by the glass door of the office. He fished the key to Room 8 from his pocked as he walked to the counter. He dropped the key on the counter.

"Tony" shrugged. "Room is paid for week. Yes? You can go."

He looked at the TV again.

Ash opened the envelope and riffled through the collection of fresh twenty-dollar bills inside, causing "Tony" to look at him again. Ash picked the one off the top and put it on the counter by the key.

"I need you to call me a cab."

"Tony" reached for the twenty, but stopped when Ash put his hand on it again.

"Preferably a cab that can get here before Detective Marand. I'm assuming you already called him."

"Tony" shrugged again, then took the twenty. "Uber is OK? Yes? I get better kickback."

It was Ash's turn to shrug. He watched as the man reached under the far side of the counter and came up with a phone. He continued to watch as the man made the call for the cab. Or the Uber. Whatever that was.

"Thanks, 'Tony,'" he said when the call ended.

"Why you always say my name like that? My name *is* Tony. Yes?"

Ash shrugged again. "Fine. Tony."

"Yes," Tony said with a short nod. "Is better."

When the car arrived, and he saw it wasn't Detective Marand, Ash went out to meet it. He carried the umbrella and his bag and threw them into the back seat before climbing in after them.

"Bus station," he told the driver, running his fingers through his hair in an attempt to make it less rain soaked.

The driver frowned at him, but only said. "I didn't know people still went to the bus station."

"Sometimes it's the only way out of town."

19

ASH WATCHED THE starred lights of the city through the rain-streaked window. The bus had left the station and pulled immediately onto a highway on-ramp. It picked up speed in the thin evening traffic, then slowed down again to merge onto another, bigger highway, Interstate 10.

While waiting for the bus to leave, Ash had figured out how to wrap his umbrella back into a compact, waterproof club, so it and his plastic bag of clothes took up very little space by his still-damp, sneakered feet.

The bus was crowded with men and women, many of them young enough he figured they must still be in college. They were dressed much like he was, in souvenir tee-shirts and sweatshirts, carrying totes and plastic bags, some with multiple strings of pink and green plastic beads around their necks. The smells of stale sweat and stale beer and stale fried cooking permeated the thick air of the bus. Their bodies radiated heat that added to the heaviness, but Ash appreciated the muggy atmosphere.

He managed something that looked like a smile in his reflection. He had made it. He was leaving New Orleans, on his way to Oklahoma—or wherever—via Baton Rouge and other cities whose names no longer meant anything to him.

The man sitting next to Ash had a tablet propped on his lap, watching a local news and weather broadcast, listening in silence on a pair of tiny ear buds. The bright screen also reflected in the window, and showed a reversed map of the Gulf Coast overlaid with a swirling mass of green and yellow and red centered over New Orleans. Ash couldn't hear what the weatherman was saying, but he could guess.

He looked past the tablet's reflection to look out at the city again. The rain was coming down in rolling, wind-pushed sheets that crashed against the side of the bus like storm swell on a levee. He didn't need a local weatherman to tell him it was raining, or that it would be raining for a long time. Maybe the entire trip back to... wherever he was going.

The gray sky overhead lit up with a crawling display of lightning followed a few seconds later by thunder. The bus picked up more speed, and the thunder and lightning seemed to fall behind. Maybe the bus would outrun the storm.

A change in color drew Ash's attention back to the tablet screen. He stared at a picture of James Rémy Derouen—the man smiled at the camera in a business suit in front of a light blue background—for a long second, remembering the man standing over him, talking down at him, telling him an impossible story—

He turned to face the screen directly. His hands twitched in his lap.

The still image was replaced by a video of a dirty, disheveled James Derouen. Bright lights illuminated the man's face, highlighting the dirt on his face, the bags under his eyes, and the confusion in his expression as he looked around. His eyes moved constantly, never resting on anything for more than a few seconds. The video showed only the man's face and shoulders, but an EMT's blanket had been wrapped around him. Flashes from cameras off-screen caused the man to blink and turn away, looking elsewhere with each bright explosion. His mouth moved, but he seemed to be saying the same thing over and over. Ash couldn't read his lips, except one word: *Jamie*.

Then, beneath the man's face, he saw the caption, "James Derouen Found Alive!"

"Hey!" said the passenger next to Ash, and pulled the tablet away from Ash's attempt to take it. To get a closer look. To hear what the man was saying about Jamie.

"I'm sorry," Ash said. "I just... I need to..." He pointed at the tablet screen. The man moved it away again. "Can you rewind that? I need to know what he's saying."

"This guy's been missing for a week," the man said, nodding at the screen. "Everyone thought he was dead, but then he shows up naked, out in the swamp somewhere."

"He was dead," Ash said. He didn't add, *I watched him die.* Before the man could respond, though, he asked, "What is he saying?"

"Nothing that makes any sense—"

"What is he saying?"

The passenger looked at him sideways, his lips in a tight line, but he pulled the headphone jack free. The tablet's tiny speakers came to life with the voice of James Derouen.

"—Jamie. I have to find her. My daughter. Jamie. Where is she?" He stared out of the screen and his eyes met Ash's. "I need her."

Another voice said, "We've contacted your daughter, Mr. Derouen. Can you tell us what happened? Were you abducted?"

"Ah, come on, man," said the passenger as Ash stood.

Ash sat back down. He stared at the screen until the image of James Derouen vanished, replaced by a pair of well-dressed news anchors.

He wanted to sit back, to let the bus carry him away. Out of New Orleans. Away from Jamie. To protect her. From the alligator god that saw her as a withheld sacrifice. To protect her from himself.

He noticed the sound of the rain on the roof of the bus had dwindled. What thunder he could hear was falling farther behind.

The god was letting him go. He would no longer be a threat to Jamie. All he had to do, was never come back—

But if he left, who would protect her from her father?

Had the god resurrected James Derouen the same way he had resurrected Ash? And for the same purpose?

"So you're done?"

Ash realized the man was talking to him. He nodded.

He reached down between his legs to grab his bag and umbrella, then stood.

"Ah, come on, man."

Ash remained standing, looking down at the man. He waited until the man twisted in his seat to open a path to the aisle.

"Where are you going, man? The bus is full."

Ash ignored the question and walked up the aisle toward the bus driver.

The bus driver glanced at him in the mirror and said, "Sir, you need to take your seat."

It took five minutes and five twenty-dollar bills from the envelope Jamie had given him to convince the bus driver to pull over and let Ash out on the side of the highway.

The storm caught up with them as soon as the bus slowed down.

Ash stepped off the bus. He was soaked in the few seconds it took him to unwrap and extend the umbrella over his head. The cold water leached the warmth out of him. He didn't even notice when the bus pulled back into the traffic and left him behind. He only had one thought, but it was enough to keep him walking, one foot in front of the other, back along the route the bus had taken.

He had to find Jamie. To protect her. From her father. And from himself.

Above him, the lightning flashed and the thunder laughed at him with a mighty roar.

20

ASH KEPT WALKING along the side of the road, clutching his useless umbrella, until a pair of headlights slowed and swerved into his path, stopping in front of him. The car honked at him, but he ignored it. He walked around the car, on the passenger side, in the gap between the car and the safety railing of the raised highway.

The passenger door opened behind him as he came even with the red taillights.

"Damn it, Ash, get in the car."

Ash turned and saw Detective Marand's head leaning out of the open door. The detective had crawled across the front seat to open the door and get his attention.

A gust of wind tore the umbrella from his hand and he watched it fly away. Then he walked back to the open door of the car. He had to wait for the detective to crawl back to the driver's side before he could get in. He pulled the door shut. Inside the car was warm, but not as warm as the bus had been.

"What the hell, Ash?" The detective pulled his seat belt over his shoulder and clicked it into place. "They said you got on the bus to Baton Rouge."

116

Ash nodded.

"So? What the hell?"

"I can't leave," Ash said. He looked at the detective. "Jamie needs me. He's back."

The detective nodded. "I wondered if you had heard the news yet. I figured that was maybe why you had left, him not being as dead as you thought."

"He was dead."

"Well, he's not now."

Ash nodded.

The detective grunted. He put on his turn signal, then put the car back in drive.

"I hope you all didn't trash your room when you left," the detective said as they pulled into traffic. "Because I think you're going to be there a while longer."

Ash nodded. "I can't leave."

THE END
of
"Alligator, Room 8"
(Gator-man #2)

About the Author

Regardless of what you might have heard, David R. Michael has renounced all plans to take over the world. As he said he would do in his concession speech, David has returned to Tulsa, Oklahoma, to spend more time with his family.

To know when new books by David R. Michael are available, and get a taste of what's coming up next, sign up for David's email newsletter here: **www.gunsandmagic.com**

www.ingramcontent.com/pod-product-compliance
Lightning Source LLC
Chambersburg PA
CBHW030234180626
46810CB00008B/3128